DISCARD

WHITE BOYS   STORIES

MCKNIGHT, REGINALD 1956-

PS3563.C3833W47 1998

white boys

white boys

s t o r i e s

Reginald McKnight

Henry Holt and Company   New York

Acknowledgments

I sincerely thank the following for their help and advice, their prayers and encouragement, their friendship and love, their hard work and support. They fall in no particular order: James and Elaine Yaffe, Denice Gess, Annie Dawid, Kit Ward, Ray Roberts, Michael Honch, Hilary Masters, Dr. Mary Helen Washington, Annie Lamott, Frederick Busch, The Mrs. Giles Whiting Foundation, Keith A. Owens, Pearl and Frank McKnight, David H. Lynn, Donald Belton, Dr. James Coleman, Dianne Kelleher, Rachael Elana McKnight, and Nora J. Bellows. I guess writing isn't such a lonely business after all.

Henry Holt and Company, Inc.
Publishers since 1866
115 West 18th Street
New York, New York 10011

Henry Holt ® is a registered trademark of
Henry Holt and Company, Inc.
Copyright © 1998 by Reginald McKnight
All rights reserved.
Published in Canada by Fitzhenry & Whiteside Ltd.,
195 Allstate Parkway, Markham, Ontario L3R 4T8.

Grateful acknowledgment is made to the following publications in which some of these stories were first published: *The Kenyon Review* for "He Sleeps" and "The More I Like Flies"; *Callaloo* for "Palm Wine"; and *Story* for "Boots."

Library of Congress Cataloging-in-Publication Data
McKnight, Reginald, 1956–
White boys : short stories / Reginald McKnight.—1st ed.
p.   cm.
Contents: He sleeps—The more I like flies—Palm wine—Boot—
The white boys.
ISBN 0-8050-4829-4 (HB : alk. paper)
I. Title.
PS3563.C3833W47   1998   97-19096
813'.54—dc21

Henry Holt books are available for special promotions and premiums.
For details contact: Director, Special Markets.

First Edition 1998

DESIGNED BY PAULA R. SZAFRANSKI

Printed in the United Stated of America
All first editions are printed on acid-free paper. ∞

1   3   5   7   9   10   8   6   4   2

For Bonnie, Leslie and Skip

contents

white boys

he sleeps

i

The muezzin's midday call floats overhead as my friend Idrissa and I wait along the roadside for the number 7 bus which we'll take to Dakar. Usually I take my lunch here in the village with the Kourmans, but today I want to be away from the village, alone with Idrissa so I can tell him about this trouble I've been having since the Kourmans moved into my place. I've been in Senegal 134 days, and it's clear to me there are things in this country I may never get used to: the cold showers, my perpetual nausea, mosquitoes and flies, the taste of the food, the insects scuttling my sleeping legs at night, the heat—we've been outdoors less than five minutes and already my clothes are rubbery with dampness, my socks gummy. Today, the sky is so piercing a blue it hums like wind on wire, so blue that Idrissa's pupils contract to nothing. The road is all the blacker in his irises. The sunlight shimmers on every surface—road, stone, the wind-bent back of the tall grasses behind us, Idrissa's coffee black brow. The sea is a rim of yellow-white foil in the distance ahead, its brightness so intense I shut my eyes for a moment and sigh in relief. The air smells of hot grass and tar, Idrissa's limy aftershave.

All of this, the air and sun, should be bracing, even stimulating, but I can't wake up. I am still in last night's dream, which I am describing to Idrissa in this way:

"I was somewhere in southern Colorado, about thirty or forty miles from where my folks live, you know? driving my sixty-seven Volkswagen Beetle—when all of a sudden the car died. I got out and pushed it to the side of the road. I walked for miles until I came to an old garage my sister's husband owned. But he was different from what he is in real life. In the dream he was as tall as you and built like a weight lifter—thighs like boughs, arms like American footballs. You ever seen American football?"

Idrissa gives me one of those looks that says, "You think we Africans live in trees?" Mouth crumpled into a smirk, eyebrow arched. "All right," I say, "Don't get huffy. I'm just asking.

"So anyway, in real life Bradley, my brother-in-law, is a bit of a pud—a weakling, you see? beer gut and everything, but here he is, huge and handsome, and, of all things, a mechanic. So I told him about my car troubles, and he nodded and nodded, folded his arms and nodded some more, but he asked me no questions. Then, before I even finished telling him what I thought was wrong with the car, he turned from me and went into the garage. Then out he came with a box full of hardware junk, you know, wires, screws, tools, brackets, etcetera, and walking out with him was my other brother-in-law, Barry Mack, who looked exactly as he does in real life: glasses, ochre skin, pointy ears."

I pause for a spell, and study Idrissa's two-toned shoes, a creamy eggshell, a caramel tan. He shifts his weight from foot to foot. Am I boring him? Does he have to piss? He slips his long fingers into his pockets, jingles his change, and removes a pack of Lucky Strikes. He's been smoking Luckies from about the time he started working for me. He says it's easier to smoke what I smoke. He lights two cigarettes, and squints at me as he passes me one. "Good idea," I say. "Hey, Idi, is this boring?"

"Go on," he says.

I do.

"We piled the junk and ourselves into an old Ford pickup and drove down the road, but the road got more and more rugged, full of deep pits and huge stones. It wasn't at all the same road I'd walked, and the distance seemed a great deal farther—and I said so, but Bradley kept insisting that he knew where the place was. But the road got worse—so bad, in fact, that we decided it would be better to leave the truck and travel on foot. Bradley pointed, and said, 'It's just over them hills.' But I looked ahead, and there was this enormous mountain range of blue-green glass, and Idrissa, man, I tell you it looked completely unassailable. I told my brothers-in-law no way should we even think about it, but they both laughed and Barry Mack said it wasn't nearly as tough as it looked.

"Okay, so we hiked, and at first it wasn't that bad. The elevation rose so gradually that it seemed almost level. The weather was clear, temperate. But little by little, the land grew strange. There'd been trees before—lodge poles, firs, ponderosas, aspen, but they gave way to twisted, stumpy things with hardly any needles and exposed roots that looked like veins. The air began to feel humid, the trail steeper, and, like, alarmingly narrow until it was barely three feet across and one side of it plunged down into a deep rocky ravine, and on the other side a gorge, hundreds of feet deep, where a great huge waterfall churned. It got so that even Barry Mack and Bradley were scared, and Bradley decided it was too dangerous to carry the box of junk and he tossed it into the gorge side. The box shrunk to the size of a mustard seed, then vanished.

"Okay, so later the path broadened a bit and the gorge and the ravine receded into the distance, but suddenly we came upon this swamp that was filled, as far as the senses could go, with decay, garbage, rot, trash, stuff piled up over years and years. And the farther we traveled the worse it became, and God, did it stink. Swill so deep, so vile, that I could barely think, let alone breathe. Filth upon muck upon waste. Plastic bags full of shit, broken toys, rotting animal carcasses, human skulls. There was nowhere you could place your feet with any certainty that you wouldn't plunge hip deep, then neck deep, into all this decay. The swill sucked my shoes clean off my feet, and I felt a horrible sensation all the way up to my mouth. My brothers-in-law were neck deep in the muck, up to their chins, and I could feel what they felt, taste what they tasted, smell what they smelled.

"Finally, just when it appeared that things were hopeless, I spotted solid ground. I pulled myself onto the bank, and found a freshwater stream running alongside it just a few yards away. I rolled into the stream, washed myself and then followed the stream until it led—check this out, man—until it led me to my father's garden. It was my father's garden, man, now that's got to mean something, right?

"Anyway, I called to Bradley and Barry Mack, told them to wade to where I was. I planted my bare feet in the soil of my father's garden, and gazed at all those fruits he grows—reds and purples, yellows and greens, shapes like breasts and penises, elbows, faces, all of it bordered by marigolds and lilacs. It smelled sweet, and the clear stream ran through its center, between the collards and the yellow squash.

"I looked for Barry Mack and Bradley, but they were gone. I washed myself in the stream one more time, then walked to my parents' house . . . and, well, that's about it. I think I woke up before I actually saw my folks."

I fold my arms and look at Idrissa's two-toned shoes, cream and tan, and say, "Weird, huh?"

Idrissa has been my guide in both the inner and outer worlds of my life here in Senegal, but he makes no reply to what I've just told him. I hadn't really expected him to. I've been here 134 days, and he has explicated at least a quarter of these days for me, but we've never talked about dreams. I'm sure his surprise has much to do with his silence. He stands here smoking, squinting down the road. He's got his arm hooked behind his back like some sergeant major, says absolutely nothing. But that's all right, for what I haven't yet told him is that until the Kourmans moved into my place, I have never, ever, ever dreamed. Not ever.

The one constant, the one thing I have always depended on, until the Kourmans moved in, was my dreamless sleep. Never in all my twenty-eight years have I ever dreamed. At least I've never remembered doing so. My sleep has always been black, empty, colorless, silent—no impressions or thoughts of any kind. But from the very day that Alaine, Kene and Mammi moved in I began dreaming vivid, colorful, indelible dreams. I intend to tell Idrissa all this, but it has to be worked up to, perhaps even worked for. This is the African way, Idrissa tells me.

A metallic green van carrying tourists from the airport to the Meridien Hotel glides past us with hardly a sound. The air momentarily fills with the smell of its exhaust, and I wrinkle my nose, squint a little. It was in such a van that I met Idrissa. It was my first day here, and his last day as an airport shuttle driver. Before I came here to collect data for my latest ethnographical survey, Jewel Hefler, a colleague of mine from the University of Denver, told me it would be unwise to befriend anyone I met at the airport. She aimed her sharp nose at me and said, "They're vultures (she pronounces it "vulchaz"), the whole airport crowd. God, they even stoop like vulchaz. Wear vulcha haircuts." She told me to ride with the shuttle drivers from the airport to the village, speak little, pay them no more than fifteen hundred francs, plus a small tip, say merci, au revoir, and keep going, but Idrissa has charmed me, it seems. His English is good, he's extremely well read, he's droll, and I was intrigued by the fact that he wouldn't take a tip (the stuff of monstrous scams, Jewel would say). But if we're supposed to be serious about studying other cultures, we should investigate the real as well as the ideal. We should, from time to time, study trouble.

When Idrissa delivered me to the Masatta Samb Hotel that day, he merely helped me with my bags, shook my hand and wished me a good afternoon. When I held out the one-hundred-CFA coin, he folded his hands behind his back, nodded his head a shade and said, "It's okay, man." He turned and left. But I saw him later that day, just after he delivered a tourist couple to the hotel, and when they offered him a tip he took it. I approached him, asked him why he'd accepted their tip and not mine, and he replied, "You came to work; they came to play. People like to pay for play, not work." I liked that, added it to my compilation of West African proverbs, in fact, and invited him to have a drink with me in the hotel bar, the Blue Marlin.

We sat at a table near the center. The place was virtually empty, save for two tomato-skinned "white" men at the bar. Their utterances were furtive—gripe about Africa, no doubt— and their voices were more like the grunts of apes than the whispers of men. Idrissa looked at the men and arched his brows, but I think it was amusement that shaped his face rather than contempt. "Are you still at work?" I said. "Yes," he said, "I'm still on the clock." Then he smiled when I evinced surprise at the level of his idiom. "I take a lickin and keep on tickin," he said, then laughed, held out his palm so I could slap it. "How'd you know I came here to work?" I said.

"I've done this job a long time," he said. "I'm older than I look. I'm about thirty." He looked nineteen or twenty, and I told him so. He nodded, and said, "You got a tape recorder, and a serious camera. You got a pen in your pocket, and a valise full of writing paper. You don't wear sunglasses or got on a flowered shirt or shorts. You don't smile so much. You look sad. You look tired."

"You're good," I said.

"You're on the clock," said Idrissa.

Idrissa helped me find the apartment in N'Gor village, the place that's recently become the source of my troubles. Of course it's not Idrissa's fault, and perhaps in *his* mind none of his business, since he knows the Kourmans no better than I and had no idea anyone else would be moving into the house after I moved in. The village grapevine led him to the place—a tidy, ranch-style house with flower gardens, lots of space, but only a fair amount of light—not five minutes, by foot, from the beach, and an equal number of minutes to Idrissa's room, which is in the center of the village. He helped me negotiate the rent I would pay to Monsieur N'doye, and I was so pleased with the price, one hundred dollars a month, that I decided I'd better keep Idrissa close to me, and hired him as my administrative assistant. Idrissa has shown me good and inexpensive places to eat, and helped me get a box at the airport post office, something that foreigners can't easily do. The most important thing is that he's introduced me to practically all my informants, the older folk in the village who are full to the brim with the proverbs, folktales and sacred stories I've been trying to collect since my arrival. I'm not ashamed to say that without him I'd be quite lost here in Senegal.

It seems I'm lost once more, and once more I intend to ask Idrissa what to do. "Idi, explain something to me . . . ," I say, and then I pause, as if for effect, but to be honest, I really don't know where to begin. My head is a logjam of synaptic misfirings and false starts. How to go at this, this thing with the Kourmans? They are good to me, yet it often seems they mean me no good. Since they moved in, don't I have a family now? Kene cooks my meals, cleans my room, does my laundry, ignores me, talks about me behind my back. And Mammi, their little girl, don't I draw pictures for her? Don't I bounce her on my knee? Don't I listen to her screams as Alaine whips her for, say, wasting food? And what *about* Alaine? Aren't I thankful for someone to tutor me in French? And we have some good times together, he and I. I remember the first time we went fishing off the jetty, how we laughed like brothers, like fools when the first breaker washed our bucket of fish away, and the second one dumped a wall of water on our heads. I remember every franc he's robbed me of, how frequently he's lied to me.

And these dreams. Why these dreams? The Ila of northern Zimbabwe are fond of saying, Buttocks rubbing together do not lack sweat, and I suppose that's true. Cohabitation does often make for conflict, but I can't tell my buttocks from a bundt cake with the Kourmans. Do people cause dreams? Is dreaming like a contagious illness? It's not that I don't know people. I have family. Both parents and two sisters, an ex-girlfriend, too, but I've lived alone for nine years, and maybe I've been immune for so long it feels as though I've never had the illness. The best thing, I suppose, is to ease into it with Idrissa, tell him only a little at first, so finally, I say to him, ". . . like, the other day, last Wednesday, I was in my room, you know, doing what I always do—transcribing material, studying Wolof, writing those vain, pointless letters to Rose, and so forth, when suddenly I heard this yelling. Just screeching. It was coming from our front yard. It got more and more intense, and it started freaking me out. Thought someone was getting murdered. I really did. I left my room and walked to the foyer, and I saw Kene out front, wielding a broom and hollering at three other women who were all hollering back. Idi, I tell you, man, them girls was smokin." Idi grins. He loves it when I "speak Americaine noire."

"Of course, you know me, man, I don't know enough Wolof to fill a babe's mouth, but you don't have to know language to know hot, so I just stood where it was cool and watched, you know, hoping that no one would get violent. Didn't wanna go out there.

"No violence, though. Things petered out after about four

or five minutes, and when Kene turned back to the house, I slipped back into my room. Another five minutes went by and then there was a knock at my door. It was Kene. You know the woman—to me she's about the second most beautiful woman I know, but she was packing ugly Wednesday. She stood there and cussed me out for a good two minutes. Finger wagging, head jerking. I didn't catch many of the specifics, but I got the point. Then she slammed the door in my face and didn't talk to me for two days.

"Well, when Alaine came home from work that evening he chewed me out . . . very nicely, understand, as though he was my grandfather giving me guidance or some shit, but I could see how pissed off he was. He told me that we're a household, they and I, that we're a family. He told me I should have defended Kene.

"Defended Kene! Like how? I mean, I ask you, how . . . I mean the language thing and the—"

"Bertrand," Idrissa says, holding up a hand. It's clear he's impatient. "Bertrand, you must know that it was impossible for you, but perhaps if you had just left the house and stood in front of everyone to let them know you are there it would have been enough. The women would have gone away. Remember what old Madame Gueye taught you? She say that the tree which is not taller than you cannot shade you. I think you very much disappointed Kene that day. The women who fought with her are to respect you, you see, but they can't do it if you don't stand. When Alaine is gone, he expect you to head the household."

"I see."

"You are second because he is older by five years."

"Okay."

"But it will be well for you. Don't worry."

The bus rolls up, we board. It shakes and churns and hums until Dakar appears outside the windows. All along the way here, I've been screaming in my head, But I didn't ask to be part of anyone's family! Which is true. They moved into what was my place, not I theirs. What's all this You-are-second-'cause-he-is-older-by-five-years jism? Should I remind Idrissa of the evening I came home and found strangers having dinner in the foyer of my house? Alaine rose from the floor smooth like a gymnast, his oily skin and his glasses shining under the yellow light. He forked over his hand, said, "Hey, welcome home," and invited me to dine. Should I remind Idrissa of my resentment when I discovered that Kene and Alaine were renting that large, airy, sunny bedroom I'd originally wanted, the room the landlord told us belonged to an itinerant German artist? There'd been no German artist. I wonder about reminding my friend, but he knows these things. Maybe I'm being too territorial, suffering some "American illness," as Idrissa would put it. I guess I'm not being very African, because I want solitude. I'm used to it. And I want dreamless sleep. I'm used to that, too.

As we disembark, I say to Idrissa, "So what do you think the dream means?"

Idi frowns. He cocks his head. "Dreams always mean the same thing," he says. "Means you're asleep."

Still on our way to lunch—on foot now—we see a woman begging on the corner of Lamine Gueye and a street I don't know. I start at the appearance of her skin. It's like a freckled apricot, sun-dried, sour, bruised. I say vitiligo, age and sunburn. My friend says she's a leper. Her fingers splay, then cup, reach out as we make our way to her. A thousand rags walk by, but she wants me. She's hungry. I reach into my pocket and take one hundred francs, breathe heat and motor oil, noon-warm goat leather, brine, the smell inside my own nose. I feel the white walls of the city settle on my shoulders. The city flits through my peripheral vision in bursts of color. "This enough, Idi?" I say, and he says, "Up to you." I bend down low to drop the coin. I study every fissure, line and curve of her oak palm. The coin burns yellow-green there in her hand, then boom! it's gone, her hand's snapped closed, and we move on. A taxicab swoops round the corner we're headed for; it tumbles on and vanishes. Abruptly, four boys, looking like a thousand, accost me, encircle me like satellites, hands upthrust like sun-shrunk leaves on branches worried by wind. " 'Mericain brudah, you godt mawney? You godt mawney, toubobie?" They're not poor; even I can see that. Western clothed and Bata shod, they drip oil milk fat honey. They saw me coming before I even heard of Dakar. And they want me, being hungry. "Idi," I say, "How do I lose these guys?" Up to me, he says. Let's go eat, he says.

i i

We start the meal with braised whitefish, crisp fins, skins and tails. There's crumbly rice as white as the teeth that glow from a black girl's mouth. I tip my head and swallow from the circle of a lemon bottle's lip, squint the fizz from my nose, and say to Idrissa, "How's Colette?" But I'm thinking of something altogether different. I'm thinking about this silly nonsense with the chicken last night. I'm thinking of dreams.

"Still in France," says Idrissa, "but when she get back I'm going to dress sharp, wear good cologne, sing pretty to her, like Marvin Gaye. She will fall down dead, I think." Idrissa is quite the killer, but I caution him about the singing. "You couldn't carry a tune in a milk wagon," I say. I take another sip from the bottle, caress it with my thumb. Idrissa looks at me for at least fifteen seconds before he says, "How is your Rose?" Then he glances over my shoulder, then down at the table, flicks a fly off the salt cup. "My Rose isn't really my Rose anymore, I guess. Didn't I tell you about the letter I got from her back in October?"

"Nope."

"Said she couldn't trust me anymore, said it was over. All the cologne and Marvin Gaye in the world won't save *my* ass. It's over . . . I guess."

"Thought you were getting married."

"Not today. Hey, let's get off this shit. Something I wanna ask you." But before I do the waiter brings our salads in two Chinese bowls. It looks extraordinarily appetizing. The sharp green bed of lettuce, the soil-sweetened carrots. My eyes go hazy at the sight of the bloody beet. The radish as red as a rash on the back of a white girl's knees. "Idi," I say, "why on earth would someone truss up a live chicken and leave it behind the couch outside my bedroom?" If my question has taken my friend by surprise, he doesn't show it. He eases his fork into a beet round, raises the beet to throat level and says, "It's a way of weaking the mind of someone so he will give you anything you ask him for." He pauses to eat the root, then says, "Who do you think put it in there?"

15

"Who the hell knows? The front door's never locked. I walk into that place, and God knows what I'll find. My landlord's kid brings his friends into our living room all the time to throw these friggin' dance parties when they think we're all out. Maybe they check with the Kourmans, but no one says squat to me—"

" 'Squat' to you?"

"It means 'nothing,' sort of."

"Two negatives."

"Skip it. My point is I have no idea what to expect. Last Sunday I found one of Monsieur N'doye's goats in the goddamn living room. The thing about the goat is I'm sure it wandered in by itself, but the chicken—"

"Berdt, whoever put that bird in that place lives in the house. I guarantee you." He pokes his fork at me. "I guarantee you."

"Idi, I don't think so. Hey, you want the rest of my salad?"

"Quoi? Doh lekk?"

"No, I don't think so—the chicken, I mean—because Alaine and I both heard the bird clucking at the same time, and searched for it together till we found it under the couch. Under it or behind, I can't remember, but he seemed genuinely surprised to find it. He was pretty upset, seemed to me."

"He was angry?"

"Sure. Looked like it."

The waiter shuffles up and scoots a small plate of tjebudjin from the edge to the middle of our table. He smiles with all eighty-eight teeth. "You are Americain?" he says.

"Liberian," I say, and his smile shrinks ever so slightly. He nods a bit, and shuffles away. Idrissa has taught me, and it makes me sad, that Africans have little interest in other

Africans. When I don't want to be bothered I'm Liberian. "When did you order that?" I say.

"There's a lot you don't see, Berdt. Doh lekk?"

"Not hungry. And can the inscrutable crap, Idi, I'm not in the mood."

"Yam, man, yam! He's smiling up at you."

"If it was someone in the house it would have to have been Mammi. I can't imagine folks as sophisticated as the Kourmans doing, you know, occult shit like that."

"Regard the oily red."

"No thanks. But where would a seven-year-old get the money to buy a chicken? Do you think a kid that small could tie up a chicken? Or do you buy them like that?"

"Ah! Real tomate, deux carottes and little purple eggplant. The smell, Bertrand, she rise up to the heaven in the center of your nose."

I lay both hands flat on the table, lean forward and say, "The joke's getting stale, Idi."

Idrissa leans back in his seat and smiles. "Okay, okay, calm down." He puts down his fork, takes up his spoon and digs into the fish and rice. I look out the window, can see nothing but the inside of my head. A field of dust balls, hair balls—gray, fuzzy. I'm not hungry. No. "Idi," I say, "I can't say I actually know the Kourmans, but it doesn't seem to me that people who were educated at the Sorbonne, that people who are Marxists, that people who're atheists—

"Hey, do you think a bound chicken can make you dream?"

"Sleep makes you dream, Berdt. Sleep."

iii

"The wrongdoer forgets, but not the wronged."
"He who cultivates in secret is betrayed by the
  smoke."
"A crime eats his own child."
"Everything forbidden is sweet."
"The heart cannot hold two."

A Jewel is not a Rose, but I saw Jewel more often, since she was my office mate, and Rose, an M.A. candidate at Colorado College, lived sixty miles away in Colorado Springs. And Jewel loved bruisingly loud rock music, she tolerated my smoking, she had a wide soft mouth, always wet, always red, that gushed obscenities, vitriol, wisecracks, gossip. She was stunningly neurotic, inexplicably angry. Very much Rose's opposite in every respect. Each morning she would stomp into the office with some new complaint about her husband's boorish manners, or how the stingy Denver air made her a living mummy, or how the department chair had stolen her ideas about reorganizing the department, or her salary, her hair, her digestion, her car. It may have been her anger, her rage, the very heat that shimmered from her that stirred me so. Her nipples were perpetually erect, her throat and chest remained perpetually flushed. Her eyes, the color of lime slices, always gazed at me with predaceous intensity. She wasn't what I thought of as beautiful, but magnetic, galvanic.

When I was with her, I would somehow bend myself to the contours of her personality in the same way light bends to the contours of a celestial body of great mass. I joked more, swore with greater vigor, gossiped as though I'd been born to do so. There were times when I would even hear myself speak in her Queens accent: "vulcha," "culcha," "wattah," "Denvah." She hated so many people, I felt honored to be her friend. Being in her presence was like being on speed.

In our one and only night in bed, she bit, scratched, snorted, cursed, drooled, put her tongue and fingers anywhere she pleased, directed me as though I were an athlete, or a slave. She even slugged me a couple times while in the throes of orgasm. When it was over she cried as though it was I who had abused her, cried as though she'd spent the night under the torment of demons. I held her, tenderly stroked her freckled face, her auburn hair, as she convulsed and coughed and howled. I felt helpless, even alarmed, for I thought that maybe she was ill. My heart rocked so violently that my upper body spasmed as though I were moving to a bass beat. Finally, when she gained some measure of composure, I calmed myself enough to ask her what was the matter. She rolled to face me, kissed me on the lips and said, "I think I'm in love with you."

"Truth is greater than ten goats."
"Lies, though many, will be caught by truth as soon as she rises up."
"Scandal is like eggs; when it is hatched it has wings."
"Shame has watchmen."
"The truth, even though it be bitter."

"Would you have told me," Rose said, "if I hadn't overheard the message?"
"I guess."
"You guess."
"Well, I don't know. It was just that one time, but she acts

as though we were betrothed or something. Goddamn, Rosie, she's married! I just figured it was some little—"

". . . hate when you call me 'Rosie.' Stop calling me—"

". . . dalliance for her. I never thought—"

". . . used to call me that, and I always hated it, and you know it. So just don't, okay!"

Her arms were crossed; her legs were crossed there on my little blue couch, and there were no tears in her eyes, no blush behind the olive in her cheeks. She bobbed her leg up and down, glared at the cow skull on the end table, or at the lamp next to it, or at some place where people like her see visions of the future, or see their own pain hovering like a hazy red globe somewhere in the air. I wanted to take her small hands in mine, press my nose against her throat, weep, beg for her forgiveness, but I couldn't. I didn't feel guilty, just exposed. "I'm sorry," I said.

"For what? Sleeping with Jewel or calling me Rosie."

"Both, I guess."

"Still you're guessing." She closed her eyes for a moment, and sighed. When she opened them again, she was staring right at me, looking at me as though she'd never seen me before, as though I were a creature she had never even imagined seeing. Her face seemed on the verge of something definable, but for me, it remained unreadable. There was nothing clear about it, neither anger, nor regret, nor disgust, nor blithe indifference. She stopped her leg-pumping and looked so deeply into my eyes, I blinked and looked at her sneakers. "Tell me something, Bert," she said. "Do you have even the vaguest idea of what I feel? Guess if you have to, but tell me, do you?"

I felt around in my head for anything that would come my

way. Anything. I knew that if I answered what I usually answered whenever she tried to penetrate me so, namely, You feel bad, she might have kicked me in the head. I thought and thought, but nothing would come. I felt as though I couldn't breathe, as though I would ossify in my uncertainty and break into a thousand pieces, but all that would come to my mind was, You feel bad, You feel bad, You feel bad. What more was there?

Finally, she sighed once more, unfolded her arms and patted the cushion next to her. "Come sit by me," she said. And when I did, she rested her body against mine, laid her right hand on my chest and said, "I forgive you, Bertrand. I forgive you."

> "It is sleep that makes one like the wealthy."
> "What gives pleasure when going to sleep is answered
> when waking."

iv

I often fall asleep to the sound of the Kourmans fucking. They're at it tonight, in fact. They fuck like newlyweds. Kene shrieks like nothing I've heard. She keens, she wails like violent weather. The first time I heard it I thought I was hearing the yowl of a panther, and my blood tore through my body, my heart shattered like glass. There is terror in her voice, and love, too. In my head I see Alaine plow deep inside her, sparking an ancient ribbon of nerves that few men seek or even unwittingly find. Nerves that stretch out tight like the belly of time. It arouses me, unstrings me. It makes me dream. Tonight as my

African brother and sister, my cousins, my parents, whatever, have sex, I plunge into sleep, and rise from it, in this tiny dark room, with these images in my head.

I invited Rose Gordon, the woman I love, but who's not in love with me, for dinner. Rose and her brother Mike, actually. The two of them discovered my deepest darkest secret: that I ate human flesh. I don't remember whose, how often, how much. But I do remember the sandwich, its meat sliced from the flank of some body on the kitchen table. I ate the hamlike flesh—fatty, meatpink, cold, as I crouched in the kitchen door while my friends drank wine in the living room. When Mike and Rose found me, I slunk out the kitchen entrance and into the living room. Later, I went back to the kitchen, and my friends were gone, but my sister, Rita, her lover Chloe, and my niece Syria were there, gazing with disgust at the body. Chloe berated me for being a cannibal. Or at least that seemed to be the reason for her criticism at first, but later it came out that she thought I was boring, and that I was creepy, that she had never liked me, nor could she imagine ever liking me, that she and Rita should keep Syria away from me. Rita defended me, but Chloe would not be moved. I hid in the bathroom until they left. And when they did I stepped into the middle of the kitchen that was now a pizza parlor.

I approached a black man wearing a red beret and looking at me with sad bloodshot eyes. He sat at my table as if waiting to be served. "You're in my way," he said, and pointed in the direction to which my back was turned. I spun round, and saw there was a stage upon which Diana Ross and the Supremes were singing "Love Child." Diana danced lewdly. Even lay on the floor, opened her legs and fingered herself. She moved across the floor, supine, knees drawn up to her shoulders, rolled as if on wheels. I stiffened like a bull. Suddenly I noticed that Ross was no longer wiry, brittle, bony, but took on the voluptuous hips, breasts and lips, the broad shoulders, the almond eyes of Kene, and we made love right there on the floor. She began to make those godawful noises. I tried to shush her because I knew the man at the table was Alaine, and I thought that if I could keep her silent he wouldn't notice us. But Alaine tapped me on the shoulder, and I started so violently I awoke.

I awakened frowsy, sweaty, hot, rank, bitter, horny, pissed off. It was as if I'd been washed up on the shore of someone else's consciousness. I am surprised to find myself still here. I dress in my underwear and sandals, take cigarettes and matches, leave my room. I step into the living room, cross to the foyer. I stand outside Kene and Alaine's door, listen to the rattle of their sleep for a moment, then step outside. It is still as the moon, but not as quiet. My ears fill up with cricket trills, the whir of frogs, the hiss of cicadas, the heavy thrum of night, which rumbles just beneath hearing. I look up at the stars and find Orion, gaze at him till my cigarette burns to the filter. I go back into the house and again stand in front of the Kourmans' bedroom door. It's still quiet in there, but this time, too quiet. I sense they are awake. And sure enough, I hear Alaine mumble something, and his wife mumble something in reply.

I believe I have this thing for Kene.

V

I am both asleep and awake, hallucinatory with weariness. Hungry, too. I lie here burning, for the Kourmans are at it again. My eyes snap themselves shut. Abruptly, I am in flight, thirty-seven thousand feet in the air. The plane's body is a hollow sausage, held aloft by spatula wings. I dream that I'm dizzy with insomnia, rigid with hunger. I know that I am back in bed, dreaming—and dreaming, I am awake. Both asleep and awake. This is why I hate dreaming. I am miles high, no sense of movement, listening to the talking man, a journalist, I think. But I'm afraid his words, at times, are warped by the wash of chemicals, the enzymes, the hormones that pull me toward a second sleep. Sleep inside sleep.

The journalist's features appear to me in disjointed flashes. They never fall together. Wide nose festooned with freckles, tired catgreen eyes, rust beard, small ears, short 'fro, small feminine hands. He says, "Ever been there before?" He points to the floor and I can see through the glass bottom of the fuselage. Out the windows it is still black, but below, I can see everything, the ocean, the crisscross of roads, vegetation tightly woven as moss. "Been here more than I can count, my man," he says. "What you see depends on where you go. . . . Folklore, huh? Well, you gonna learn more than folklore, I'll bet." He pauses, squints at me. "So I guess you'll be living in the villages and whatnot, huh?"

I tell him I don't know, but that I'll contact people at the University of Dakar, and maybe the embassy, too. "Screw embassy people," he says. "I know embassy people; ain't worth the time. Plantation mentality. Neocolonialists. They're the last ones you wanna ask about Africa. Strike out on your own. Take it in; drink it up. You'll like it. Can't help but. It's home, homey. Drink deep, young man. What you see depends on where you go. Lemme show you." He points to the floor and says, "Look how the colors squeeze tears from your eyes. All those people in lemon, saffron, watermelon, cobalt, gold, kelly, scarlet. Listen to 'em laugh; see their ivory teeth; listen to the sounds of Citroëns, Subarus, Muslim prayers, buses, car rapides; smell the cattle, the spermy ocean; feel the thunder of dance; breathe the ochre dust; talk politics with that group of khaftan-clad men.

"Yeah, I'm going to Banjul to cover the coup. You hear about the coup? Yeah, Jawara's out on his ass. Outta there." Look at those spiders, he says; taste those citrons, those guavas, those little bananas; wear that grass green boubou; chew that kola nut; smoke those Lucky Strikes; steer clear of those military men; eat that snow white rice. He points out thing after thing, and I can taste it, hear it, see it, smell it, feel it all. It's exhausting—poverty, palm trees, Brahma bulls, millet, gyros, pot. The people. Polyrhythmic drums and koras. Cafés, fetid jail cells. Cornrowed women, soccer games, reggae, soul eaters, Bata stores. Fresh fish, sweet clams, Gauloises and Etoile de Dakar. Chickens bound tight as electric coils, goats, turkeys, baboons. He does go on.

And he's not the only speaking traveler, now. There is this woman, too. A big beige woman in lime green leisure, hair the color of ginger, blood fingertips. Luggage-large hips and thighs, a voice to bore holes through rock, a mole beneath the eye. She means to whisper, says, "Baby, you just don't know," says, "Them niggers sure can do," says, "Got dicks as big as wrists," says, "And black? Real black like lava stones," says, "tar pits, mine shafts, belts and heels. Not that faded shit you see in Jersey. Make a woman out you, darlin' dear."

"Whut we gwine do," breathes the journalist, " 'bout loud-moufin cullid folk like dat dar." I try to smile, but it feels more like a wince. He scrapes his beard, just so, with index and middle fingers. He sniffs and says, in a perfect British accent, clipped and round and square where it ought to be, "They'll foul the continent, old man." I list toward sleep, a sleep inside sleep, and everything slides across the floor of my brain. "Yeah," I say.

"You'll like it down there," he says in his own voice. "You'll learn just who you are." And my consciousness slips with flashes of light amid gray mist. Slips with a crackling sound like power lines at night. Slips, and I dream of sleepless me.

v i

Noon.

Alaine is twenty paces from me. He's just stepped off the bus, noon lunch. It's my plan to take the bus to the airport restaurant, since I'm growing increasingly sore about the constraints of "family" life. I want to be alone. I want nothing. Alaine will certainly try to convince me to stay home for the meal. He sees me, moves right to me. He is slender, soldierlike in his stride, sunglasses, trouser creases splitting air like butcher knives. I rarely see him dressed this way. If I were curious, I'd ask him why. Velvet head cut smooth like a cue tip, goatee tight as macramé, glassy shoes, lotion thinskin glaze. And here I am, all bushes and brown rice, general unkemptness, dashiki madness, chicken-bound, weakneed. The heat suffocates me, softens me flesh to bone. I can't fight a man in these rags.

"Bertrand," he says, "where do you go? Doh lekk?" I tell him I've got errands to run in town, but he "reminds" me that nothing will be open till three, when siesta ends. "Well," I say, "the airport stores stay open from now till three."

And as he lights a cigarette, he says, "Too expensive. What you need? I get it for you tonight." He removes his shades and focuses on my chest, rather than my eyes, and he says, "You spend too much money. We have got to start being more careful with money." I slowly close my eyes, inhale, and slowly open them. I say, "I think we need to talk about—"

"In fact," he says, looking me in the eye this time, "I think I should tell you something important. Come on, I buy you what you need in town. Later." I relent as easily as I thought I would. Must be the bound chicken thing.

He leads, and I follow him across the road and past the little mom-and-pop store where I often buy bug spray, candles, canned milk and meat, cigarettes and matches; past the big locust trees and the hedge of bougainvillea; past the shanty where an old man and his son live; past the twelve-room house where the Samb family live; past the mosque, where the muezzin is now calling the devout to prayer; down the sandy path that leads to "our" place. "Listen," Alaine says, before we enter the courtyard. "Listen," he says again. "Don't, don't, don't tell Kene, but I am feared I might lose my job. I don't know of certain, but the political situation at my work is not good."

I am only vaguely aware of what Alaine does for a living, some kind of clerical work in one of the ministry offices in town. I do know that when he says "political" he doesn't mean his inability to suck up to the right people. He means that he's often held in ill regard for his national political views. He's a member of the Senegalese Democratic Party, which the dominant party, the Progressive Senegalese Union deemed (along with every other party) illegal up until the mid-seventies or so. None of the lesser parties is still thought fully legitimate or acceptable by the dominant powers, and Alaine isn't shy about expressing his views. Alaine doesn't appear to be upset in the least, but it's clear that he's more than a little concerned. "We must be careful with money until things look better," he says.

"Well," I say, "I'm pretty careful as it is. You're asking me to give more to Kene each week? Is that it?" Why am I acquiescing this way? Why can't I show him how angry I am? Here I am imagining kicking him all the way to the beach, but speaking to him in a manner almost uxorial. Me, the new Mrs. Kourman. Alaine tosses his cigarette to the ground and steps on it. "Not now," he says. "The money is same as normal for now."

"Um, that's good, see, because—"

"Things are good now. The food is inexpensive because we fish, and the rent is, for me and my wife, very good."

"Can't complain, thirty thousand CFA is extremely cheap compared to what I paid in the States. Back there I—"

He clutches me by the arm. His eyes are big. "You are paying thirty thousand?"

"Sure."

He releases my arm and raises his hand to his brow. "Wyyyy! Too much. Too much. For that little room you pay thirty thousand?"

"It's not just the room, you know, but—"

"You pay almost what we pay for the two *big* rooms." He

28

grabs my arm again and looks me dead in the eye. "You must talk to Monsieur N'doye. He charge you too much. Too, too much."

"But Idrissa told me the price was fair for, you know . . . He said the price was good. And it's nowhere near what I was paying in the U.S."

"He do this to you?"

"Idi? Sure. Yes. He interpreted for me, but he didn't set the price. It's just that, you know, compared to what I paid back home it's pretty reasonable."

"No, no, no, no, it's not. It's not reasonable at all. Idi know. He know! You must get you rent lower. He's take advantage of you. Too much. Too expensive. Idi know this. He know this." He's getting very worked up, and, of course, so am I, only we express it in diametric ways. While he paces with his head lowered, his brow knitted as if he were feeling not only disgust, but pain, I stand here motionless, watching his squat shadow weave the ground like a fish weaves water. I hold my face without expression, if such a thing is possible, but my guts quiver, my teeth crack.

"Alaine! Bertrand! Come and eating!" Kene hollers from across the yard. She smiles at me as I step within a few feet of her. "I am use English," she says, smiling as pretty as love itself.

v i i

Dear Rose,

I try particularly hard, these days, to keep my letters to you brief. Since I write so frequently, I should at least try to be concise. That's real hard for me to do. And maybe I should wait for you to write me again. I shouldn't keep answering your last letter over and over again. But here I write. Can't help myself, I suppose.

Rose, I don't understand this "great love" I have for you any more than you do. Though it might seem so, though I might even fear it sometimes, it isn't obsessive. Overbearing maybe, too late perhaps, maybe even bizarre, and clearly one-sided now, but I'm not obsessed.

For the past several months I've felt that there is some one thing I did that I could take back, or some one thing I could say. But you can't undo sex, and words are clearly not doing the deed. When I left I was so certain that you were deeply in love with me, despite what I'd done. I expected many letters from you. And I thought that each of us would do a lot of hemming and hawing, trying to figure out what we could do to straighten things out between us. It felt so good to be sitting in those airports, last summer, being paged to those white phones. It made me feel like God's buddy. My own mother wouldn't have called me at the airport, but you, Rose, you did. It made me want to write you every week. Why did you call me at Stapleton, and La Guardia, and say all those nice things, if you didn't—I don't know what to say anymore. Here I am stuck with this great love for you and I don't know what to say or do for myself.

Help me, will you? I don't even know how to write this letter. I'm in trouble here. The folks I live with, people I've lived with for the past two and a half months, seem like decent people, but I don't know if I can trust them. Same goes for my assistant, Idrissa, the guy I've been mooning over for all these months.

Good, you'll say. Serves you right. Maybe you'll know how it feels to trust, then suddenly to not trust. I don't know what I'm doing or saying in these letters to you. I'm alone here. I'm too much inside myself, too inside my head. I'd like to think that if I hadn't slept with Jewel, you'd be writing me every week, and we'd be okay, but I'm probably kidding myself. But, Rosebaby, it was just that once, and I told you about it. When you told me it didn't matter (It's not cheating if you're not married, you said), I knew you were being kind. I knew I'd pay, too. I'm paying big.

I dream now.

A few nights ago I had this dream and I want to tell you about it because I figure it might help me explain why I did what I did to you and to me. Here it is.

I was in Manhattan, and I was supposed to give this paper at some university nearby, though I don't remember the topic. It was a cloudy day and I was thinking of it as a typical N.Y. day, as if I know what that is. Well, I was nervous about being in N.Y., intimidated by the whole thing, riding subways, reading before a cigar-chewing N.Y. audience, and I freaked out and went back to my hotel. When I got back, though, it was immediately evident to me that someone had been in my room. Then it was apparent that the person was still there. It turned out it was the cleaning woman, young, tall, gorgeous, the same skin color as me, perfect build. For some foolish reason I began speaking to her with an Italian accent. We seduced each other and ended up making love on the floor. She'd never had a person go down on her, so I did, and she climaxed. I know this must be making you uncomfortable, but there's no sense in me expurgating a dream, Rose.

I dressed afterward and went to the university to give the

paper, but never actually got there. Again I went back to my hotel, and there, in my room, I found the woman and her boyfriend, a light-skinned, tall, bearded man. He told me he'd heard me speaking when I checked into the hotel, and that I certainly hadn't had an Italian accent. I tried other accents, but they weren't buying it. They said, Just speak in your own voice. I did, but they didn't seem to like it.

Then later, still in N.Y., you and I went fishing in a polluted river. The East, I guess. I selected your fly and tied it on. I showed you where to cast. You caught one almost immediately. It was a very ugly diseased fish, whose gray-white skin was falling off, whose eyes were like white beads. It smelled like rot and motor oil, and I cut your line and let it fall back into the black water.

That's pretty much it, babe. And since I'm not used to dreaming, you can't expect much from me in terms of my interpretive skills. I think it's pretty clear, though, what it means, and all I can say is I'm sorry for being what I've been, and doing what I've done. Please, please, please forgive me, if you can, and I'll speak to you in my own voice from now on, and I'll take you to clear waters, and lead you to pretty fish—rainbows, greenbacks, speckleds. We'll reel them in, and let them go. I don't ask you to love me. Just talk to me.

Already I've gone on too long with this letter. But it probably doesn't matter. I'm sure you don't read the goddamn things anymore, all this microscopic scribbling on graph paper. It must look insane. None of it makes sense, and really, I hate dreaming. But it does make you think.

Please write me.

Love,

Bert

viii

I walk the beach. I look at things. The sun's crown is brass orange on the horizon, and the ocean is coppery glass flecked, now and then, with mango, rose, violet, silver . . . actually, every color I can name if I stare long enough. It's as though the world is blank, the world is white, and from that whiteness, color and shape intermittently thrust themselves at the eyes. Watermelon, turquoise, sand, olive, cherry, sand. Sometimes white wings shred themselves from the air in a great flock, swirl and loop and dive. They might become a great amoeba, then a cloud. Salmon, pearl, forest, peach, butter, tar, sand. Four large pelicans rise from the strand, like mushrooms, huddle on the darkening beach like hoodlums. I look at them, I look at everything, really, as though I mean to collect them, store them away till I can better see and understand them while I sleep. Sand, smoke, cherry, grape, lemon, sand. Take them to the black wall of sleep, hold them up as you would hold cleary marbles between your eye and the light. It makes more sense to me now. Seeing, hearing, tasting, touching, smelling make more sense now.

As I near the pelicans, I hear Idrissa call my name. I stop, but don't turn toward him. I don't move. I watch the pelicans. I watch the seagulls. I close my eyes and see odd things, unfamiliar things, things from future dreams. I open my eyes, and turn to see Idrissa galloping toward me. It strikes me odd to see him running, never having seen him run before. Idrissa ambles, he plods, he lopes, on occasion he even struts, but run, no. I turn away from him and gaze at the four hoodlums again. Perhaps in the clear black of the night they will be four witches at the cauldron, or a snowstorm on the beach. Perhaps I'll carry one on a subway, or eat her eggs, or run in terror from her. Whatever she'll be, however I'll see her, she'll be no less real than what she appears to be in clear light, for she'll be shot through with me, my needs, my fears, my memories. My bird. My creation. Mine.

Idrissa claps a hand on my shoulder and says, "You need to go home." He sounds excited and sad and weary, all at once. Despite my desire to tell him to screw himself, I turn and say, "Some tribe somewhere on this continent, my good buddy, says something like, 'Home is not where I am born, but where it goes well for me.' In my case, I'd say, 'Home is not where I live, but where I live alone.'"

Idrissa folds his arms over his chest, and jerks his head toward the village. "It's a bad time for proverbs, Berdt. You should come." And I do, despite myself. I cannot, for some reason, maintain my resentment. Dreams must melt resentment. I suppose that's because what we see in the clear light is only half of what is to be. There's nothing and no one to judge until we have slept on things.

i x

Kene slaps Alaine so hard his eyes tear up. Her Wolof snaps through the room like a ricocheting bullet. Alaine slaps her left ear twice. He's been smiling, but his smile is only half there, on the lower part of his face, masklike. His red eyes glare hard, sharp, semimurderous. Again he slaps her twice on the left ear, and grabs her arms, which are chopping hard. Alaine tries to pin both her arms under his left arm, and tries to slap her again, but Idrissa wedges himself between them, and folds his arms around Alaine. I see that Alaine is bleeding beneath one eye, and fingernail welts run from his left ear to his beard. There's no time for asking what's caused all this, no real way to gain purchase on the flying arms, but I lay my hand on Kene's shoulder, and before I can say, It's okay, it's okay, calm down, she spins, knees me in the balls, and arcs across the room as I go down. I see the tan soles of her feet, the multicolored pagne skirt blur to a brownish haze as she makes her way. She plucks an empty wine bottle off the sideboard, spins round and hurls herself back toward Alaine, who won't take his eyes off his wife or relinquish the terrible half smile. In my mind, I'm asking Idrissa, What's going on? What's this all about? But there's no time.

I feel myself rise from the floor and tackle Kene as she crosses in front of me. Her warm, soft fleshiness, her ball-sapping strength, her perspiration. The bottle scatters its green wash across the floor, and my elbow and forearm are bitten by green teeth. Kene rolls away and rises. Alaine breaks away from Idrissa, and husband and wife tumble into each other, scratching, slapping, cuffing, tugging, ripping. Idrissa grabs at Alaine's right arm, misses, grabs for his left. Alaine twirls and pulls away. He dashes to the foyer and out the door. Kene lunges after him. Idrissa and I follow only to the door and no further. We watch them plunge into the night. I turn, as if by instinct, and I see Mammi, the little one, sucking on the second knuckle of her index finger. Her face is wet with tears, but she is silent. I approach her, reach for her, but she backs away. "I'll get Madame N'doye for her," says Idrissa, and he steps out the house.

X

The house is quiet now, and I am in bed. I'm crushed with fatigue, and Kene's belt to my testicles—and the poor meal I shared with Idrissa tonight—make my stomach queasy and liquid feeling. My elbow and forearm burn, and I'm sure there's still glass to be plucked from them. Of course there had been no dinner tonight, so I walked to the mom-and-pop store with Idrissa to buy fruit, canned meat and bread. We took our time going there, and took our time returning. Somewhere between the course of going and coming, Idrissa told me that the fight had had something to do with Kene's anger over Alaine's Belgian mistress, and his dismissal from his job. When we returned, we found the Kourman family, and Kene's best friend, Oumi Samb, sitting on the porch silent and sullen. We made no greetings, and no one greeted us. Kene was dressed in rather formal attire, boubou, head wrap, newish sandals. Oumi was dressed similarly. It was clear that Kene had every intention of leaving. Idrissa sat with them, but I walked inside the house. I saw two suitcases. I turned toward the door, and said, "Idi, may I have a word with you?"

I wasn't angry, and I had no idea what I was going to say to him. Idrissa stood and joined me inside. I nodded to the couch, and we sat down heavily as old men. I sat back, crossed my legs, and then I noticed I was jittering with nervousness. "I talked to Alaine the other day," I said, "about the arrangement you helped me make to get this room." I pointed my thumb over my shoulder. "He told me I was paying too much. Way too much." I paused to let the words sink in, to read his face for signs of discomfiture, but Idrissa remained taciturn. I felt anger rise up from my belly, but before I said another word,

Idrissa folded his arms and leaned back, tipped his head to the side and said, "It was too much money for you?"

"That's not the point."

"You said it was three hundred fifty dollars lesser than what you paid in the U.S. You were happy with the price?"

"Idi, that's not my point."

He crossed his legs, stretched his arm across the back of the couch. "Tell me the point," he said.

"I guess I . . . I guess I thought we were friends."

Idrissa looked thoughtful for a moment. He squinted; he shrugged. "Sure. Sure, you and I are friends. But now I must ask you what your point is. I don't understand you."

"Alaine says I'm paying too much for the room. He said you knew that from the start. He said you should have helped me get the place for a cheaper price. That's what a friend would do, Idi . . . Goddamn it."

"The rent was not too expensive until Alaine said it was, true?"

"Wait a minute—"

"You were happy until Alaine said these things, true?"

"Idi—"

"Alaine has made you angry with your friend, true?"

"Wait a second. Wait a second—"

"With me you had peace. With Kourman you are not at peace. Why you doubting my friendship? Why you trusting a guy who would break your peace and not me?" He pointed to his chest with his right hand and turned his left hand, the one resting on the couch, palm up. The sclera of his eyes were red with exhaustion, his brow knitted. He said, "You told me that . . . that the university was paying you, and this other foundation, too, who pay you. I didn't think it was your own

37

money. You spend so much. You give to everybody. What I always tell you when you ask about money? 'Up to you; it's up to you.' " He began nodding. "Yeah," he said, "yeah, but all the time you put this responsibility on me to tell you this and that, and I keep telling you the same thing: 'Up to you.' Can I tell you everything? Am I God?"

Before I could answer, the Kourmans and Oumi entered. Kene and Oumi each took a bag. Then Kene held out her hand to Mammi and Mammi clasped that hand. But Alaine firmly took Mammi's other hand, and said in Wolof, "She stays here." Kene pulled. Alaine pulled. They jerked the child back and forth, making her head snap side to side. Idrissa rose from the couch and approached the four with his hands raised. "Not good, not good, not good," he said. I stood and entered my room, thinking, Tonight, let them be his family.

xi

As my bed whirls me toward sleep, I hear Kene shriek. I hear her wail. It is a restful, peaceful, lulling sound. We are making love with a fervor that's beyond the usual intensity. She yowls like a night creature. I hum stupidly, atonal, but rhythmic, and our bed barks, juddering across the tile floor. I'm as tumescent as a football, knocking the narrow walls of Kene in a bed of green glass. She grips me so tightly I feel the pressure round my neck, on the tip of my nose. She comes two, three, four times, and then I myself let go. Only then do I feel the sun beat down on my face, and see the green glass crushed to fine powder on Kene's breasts. I remove the pillowcase from the pillow and gently sweep the glass powder away. She brushes her index finger against the hollow at the base of my throat, collecting sweat beads under her nail, and she says, "Nothing can be given; everything must be earned. Until now, you've been only half awake. See how it goes?"

We are Chinese, though black, and we are slaves being mated by two abusive white men who run a farm high in the mountains of Colorado. Our bed is in the open air now, and a breeze cools our skin. As I dust the powder from my lover's breasts, I feel my own hands on my breasts, my penis inside me; my hands reach down to caress my face. I feel the sun both on my back and on my face, my chest. We both sit up and gaze out and away. Our overseer seems to be gone, but we are afraid to run, just now. We decide to wait till dark. Scrub pine, mesquite, pale blue sage, and tumbleweeds all around us, we see our freedom everywhere we look, for everywhere we look, we see ourselves.

the more i like flies

All right, man, so I'm busing down tables—we gotta do our own here, and we gotta sweep, mop, wash dishes and do just about everything else, too—and trying to keep flies off my arms and the sweat out my eyes and the seam of these polyester monkey suit pants from working into the crack of my ass. I ain't even gonna tell you how disgusted I am with all this wreckage these ape-neck cadets have left behind. And we gotta throw all this crap away, too. Three and a half gallons of milk, four, maybe five pounds of scrambled eggs, a whole pig's worth of bacon, enough French toast to feed France, and I'm saying to myself, like, Yeah, like I really need this crap. Up at three-goddamn-thirty in the morning, so I can drive to the Air-god-Force-damn-Academy to spoon-feed and clean up after these little dweebs. . . . Six-thirty-three-the-hell A.M., and I been at this gig for two hours already—already driven up all these hills and black curves, dodging deer and drunk airmen, to sweat into my eyes and sling chow. Love it. But then, like, from nowhere ol' Kelly, my partner, goes, "What's so great about bein goddamn white?" Hello! I say to myself. There he goes. Good ol' Kelly. But I keep my mouth shut, naturally. No sense going into it. This is Kelly.

But still, I'm thinking, How about this, ya dope: Try walking down the street at night, minding your own beeswax, and a white couple comes at you from the opposite way? and it's hot outside, so you're ambling, just ambling, and it's not all that late, just blue black with a few stars, like you like it, and you're thinking about, say, nothing really, okay? and you don't even mind the water sprinklers spitting on your right side. And the crickets sound nice, don't they? Then when Ken and Barbie get within a half block of you they cut across the street like you're a hissing viper hellhound man, bristling with Uzis and hypodermic needles. You can barely keep yourself from hollering, *Oh, come ooonnn, I gotta Korean girlfriend and my best buddy's white, and you people got to simply lay off renting so many goddamn gangsta movies. Kumbaya, baby. I'm respectable.* Pin heads. What's so great about being white is you get to act like everybody else in the world is a scary monster.

Like I say, all this I keep to myself cause once this old melonhead's got his mind made up to say something, you can't stop him. He's like a four-foot stack of plates tipped at a forty-five-degree angle. Get 'em that far gone and you can kiss a big hunk of your paycheck good-bye. That's Kelly. Soon's he opens his mouth he's already at forty-five degrees. Too late. Man says what he's gotta say. "You think we'll get our pay today?" I ask him, even though I know it won't make a damn bit of difference what I say. I look at him and see him working them bones in his temples, working 'em. You'd think he was chewing corn husks. But didn't have a damn thing in his mouth but his own words. He says, "You colored guys make it sound like don't nobody else in the world feel pain."

"Hey look, Kelly, I ain't said jack to you, man. Go talk to Mendez; he's the one pissed you off this morning."

"Move," he says, then sweeps in front of me, then behind.

I say to him, "You know, we'd get done quicker if we sweep at the same time and clear at the same time, and wipe at the—"

"Mendez don't listen." He swipes his hand through the air, stands straight and leans on his broom. "At least you listen. And Mendez gets loud, too. I can't talk to him, 'cause no matter what you say he gets loud. I can't talk to loud people."

"Do you wanna get the mop, or me?"

"A guy like that'll never learn shit. You look at him. He's supposed to be our shop steward, setting an example for younger lads like yourself, and what's he doing?"

"Same as usual, walking around with a pitcher fulla drumsticks and talking smack while he's supposed to be working."

"Fat son of a bitch."

"Yeah, well, I'll mop and you can clean the silverware and plates." I walk into the kitchen and just about drop from the heat. Jesus, how can these cooks take this nonsense? I walk past the ovens and see they're empty. They haven't even started lunch yet, I notice, and start wondering where Mendez got the chicken legs. I look for George, which is easy, 'cause he's the only one in here who wears a cloth chef's hat. Everybody else wears paper. I find him at the chopping block, skinning garlic. This is pretty much where you can expect to find

George, and that's what he'll be doing when you find him. Skinning garlic. He's got a year before he retires, so I guess no one'll say squiddly to him about goofing off.

"Georgie Pordgie. How's your old Chef Boyardee–looking ass?"

"Say, babe, what's to it?"

I don't care much for the way guys around here call each other "babe." I know they don't mean nothing funny by it, but the only person I call babe is Hwasook, my girlfriend. But lately I've been kind of joking with Ray by calling him babe. He'll walk into our apartment and I'll say, "Hey, babe," and he'll say, "Hey, babe," and we'll both get a grin out of that. We did it once when Hwasook was over and you could tell it made her uncomfortable. Even after we explained it was a joke she still didn't get it.

"Say, George, where'd Mendez get the bird legs?"

"Cooler."

"He's grubbing a whole pitcher full of cold chicken legs?"

"Microwaves 'em in Salazar's office."

"You mean Salazar don't care?"

George said he didn't care, so I said, See you George, and went back to the soap room to get the mop and bucket. I was a little twicked off about finding out that a guy like me'll get written up by Salazar for snatching a handful of shrimp while Mendez gets away with a pitcher or a plate full of whatever the hell he wants all day long. We're not supposed to eat any left-overs, but most guys do. Better not get caught, though, 'cause they will nail you, even though it takes an act of Congress to actually fire a civil servant. But Mendez does whatever he wants. Maybe it's because most everybody likes him. Maybe because he's shop steward. But it isn't because, like Kelly says, that Mendez is a "colored Mexican," and in cahoots with Salazar. Mendez'll tell anybody who wants to listen that he's Panamanian. But to me the guy's all Brooklyn. I figure a guy like Kelly, though, thinks anyone with a Latino name is a Mexican.

As far as I can see, Mendez and Salazar despise each other, and it's clear that Salazar's terrified of Mendez. Mendez knows it and loves to rub Salazar's face in it. Calls him Sally, throws an arm over the little dude's shoulders, musses his glossy pompadour. Salazar smiles back with tight white lips, and never says squat. I mean, all you gotta do is compare one to the other and you can see why. Salazar can't be taller than five foot four, and if he weighs much over one-twenty on any given day it's 'cause he's carrying his grocery money in quarters. And he's got about as much personality as he's got body weight and height. Big ol' meaty Mendez could have the dude fried up crispy, carry him around in a pitcher and munch him in maybe four quick bites. Mendez is all personality; the big, quick-stepping, fast-talking lug is everywhere at once, in sight and sound. Cahoots my butt. Mendez owns the place, and you gotta admire him, sort of. But still this chicken-in-O'-pitcher crap twicks me off and I tell Kelly about it when I get back to our section. All Kelly says is, "Proves my point." And before I can stop myself I ask him what he means, so he says, "When you finish mopping, we'll take a break."

So I sit down for break after I'm done and Kelly comes from the kitchen with the usual yogurt, the usual orange and the usual sausages. He bathes the sausages with Frank's Louisiana Hot Sauce, and as per usual asks me why I'm not eating, and as usual I tell him I don't eat breakfast. Then I say, "You know, if we don't get our checks today, I'm gonna tell Salazar to pay my rent."

"It's just like I'm saying, Scott, what's so goddamn great about bein' white?"

Hello! Anybody home? Plates, I tell you. Plates, stacked four feet high, heading straight down like a gunshot victim and there's nothing I can do.

"I mean look," he says. "You don't get your check. I don't get my check. How's my color make it any better for me?" He clicks his flat hazel eyes twice, runs his freckly hand over his crew cut, sliding his paper hat a couple notches to the left.

"Couldn't tell you, all I know is that civil service pay is supposed to be guaranteed on time."

"And do I get a tax break 'cause I'm white?"

"Nine extra days is just too damn long to wait, if you ask me. Hey, how come it's taking so long anyway?"

"Scotty. You know why I retired early from the Corps?"

I give up, so I say, "You got shot. You told me."

"Know why I got shot?" He pushes his paper hat back off his brow, then dumps salt and more hot sauce on his sausages. I tell him no I don't know why he got shot. "You know who shot me?"

"You weren't shot in Vietnam?"

Kelly stabs a sausage with his fork, pops it into his mouth and chews it so hard I can hear his teeth knock together. I wave a fly off my ear. After a minute Kelly says, "There was this kid in my company, well, not really a kid like some of the boots in my company. This lad had seven years in. Did a couple tours in Vietnam, too, but was only a private first class."

"So why'd he shoot you?"

"Did I say he shot me?"

"Well get to the—"

"No I didn't, so let me—"

"All right! All right!"

"You never listen."

"Kelly, just ten minutes ago you said . . . Okay, Kelly, you're right. I don't listen."

"They called him Barney for some damn reason, but at the inquest and the court martial they called him by his real name, but I don't remember it. Never forget what he looked like, though. This fella had one a them bull necks, built like a little oak stump. Heavy beard. Black eyes. Had eyelashes that looked like, you know, a girl's. No, I won't be forgetting that mug for a long while. The guy was Indian, but I don't know the tribe or nothing. But that's what made him wild. Mean, lazy and smart, too, I'm telling you.

"You know, I'd walk into the squad bay sometimes, for some reason or another, and I'm telling you, it'd be like ten, eleven hundred in the morning and there'd this kid be, in his boots, trousers and undershirt, just snoozing like a papoose. Course I'd wake him up and he'd tell me some kind a bull-puckie like he'd just give blood or was suffering heat stroke, or didn't nobody bother to wake him up at reveille, or like that, and I'd go, 'Well where's your med pass?' or 'Whycome you're in uniform?' or something and he'd get pissed off, get his ass up, put on the rest of his uniform and get his Indian ass to work."

Kelly sniffs and holds his coffee cup under his nose, just staring off into space. I look at his nose hairs, and his bushy knuckles, and his arms, which are fuzzy as a dog's leg, and I say

47

to myself, Well, looks like some white people got it better in winter, but I sure wouldn't wanna be you in all this heat. Kelly sniffs again and sips his coffee. "Goddamn *right* I did," he says, as if I've just said, Gosh, Kelly, really?

"But nobody else would," Kelly says. "Company commander didn't say shit, hell, his own platoon sergeant didn't say shit. I did. Good ol' Gunny Sergeant William P. Kelly did. I never understood this, Scott, I never did. Some guys seemed to respect him 'cause of all the chest cartoons he'd picked up in combat. Man, you shoulda seen that boy in dress uniform. Had a chest fulla combat ribbons, enlistment stripes on his sleeve, too, of course, but just one goddamn stripe. One." Kelly's pointing a finger in my face like I can't count. "That told me everything I needed to know. It was like he was saying to everyone, 'Lookit me, I done my time, so lemme alone and lemme collect my paycheck.' Nobody but me seemed to care. Kid wasn't even in my platoon. I was motor pool; he was comm, but you think any one a them shitbirds in the comm platoon'd say something to 'im?

"Well, one day I caught him in the rack and it was something like thirteen hundred hours in the afternoon or what have you, and so I nudge him with my foot and he sits up like a dead body'll do if it lays around a few days. Well, he says, 'What time is it, Gunny?'

" 'It's time somebody wrote you up,' I say, 'if you don't have an excuse for being in that rack, PFC.' And get this: He jumps out his rack, throws his blouse and cover on, telling me he's got an excuse, but that he's gotta go get it. Well that little son of a bitch walked out and never did come back. I wasted twenty minutes waiting for his dumb ass to come back, but he never did. Well, I was mad enough to piss fire, but I let it go. Wasn't in the mood that day, I guess."

Kelly pops the last sausage into his mouth and has some more coffee. Those little skull bones are working like he's got at least a dictionary or two worth of words in his mouth. He stares down at his plate and chews. I sit back and wait. This obviously ain't his point, though, with ol' Kelly, you just never know. The plates ain't hit the floor yet. I swipe at a fly and it vanishes somewhere past Kelly's ear. "So what's this got to do with why white folks got it so bad?" I say.

"You know, breakfast is the most important meal of the day, Scott. You oughta take advantage. Only thirty cents a meal, lad." I just hiss and shake my head. Then my heart just about pops when I'm jolted by someone's meathook slapping down solid on my shoulder. I hear, "What you boys think this is," and when I turn, I'm staring right into little Salazar's mustache, even though I'm sitting and he's standing ". . . a retirement home?" he says.

"Break ain't over yet," says Kelly. Salazar ignores him and looks at me. "I need someone to hit your section one more time with the mop, Mr. Winters. Sergeant Klutsky spilled some coffee between table five and table six."

"Someone. You mean me."

"Everybody else is eating," says Salazar, and he looks a little stunned that I'm irate. I'm not usually irate, but Kelly's kinda rubbing on my hindmost nerve.

"Hey," says Kelly, "we getting paid or not?"

"Paychecks are in my safe," says Salazar, then he scoots away on those size-six patent leather shoes of his. Damn things squeak and glimmer like a couple a mechanical toys. Kelly's looking at 'em, too, them shoes. Looks at 'em like he hates 'em. "Why's he always come to me for crap like that? He never says jack to the other new guys."

Kelly says he does it 'cause I let him. I guess that's true, but I'm new here and can't afford to act like I own the place, like I'm Mendez. I've got a month and a half of probation left. But even if I was a full civil service employee I don't think I'd play the jigaboo some of 'em expect me to. That's the kind of thing you just can't explain to an old bonebrain like Kelly. It means something different when a black guy skates at work from when a white guy does. It might not be so, but you always feel white people are watching you, waiting for you to screw up, pissed off a little if you don't. And they can't really make up their minds about us. I mean, they call you lazy, but every so often I overhear white dudes in the locker room say, "Yeah, babe, busted my ass today, worked like a nigger, I'm telling ya." But I can't make up my mind either, 'cause what I can't figure, is whether I look more like a "jigaboo" if I don't try to slide by with hardly any work, or if I kowtow to de boss man. Can't win as long as someone else calls your game, I guess. And, like, would it be okay working during break time if a white guy had asked me to? What if Mendez was my boss? Would I feel like poor old Uncle Tom then? Skip it, I tell myself. All I wanna do is keep my job for now.

I get up, stretch. "Well," I say, "by the time I get back from the soap room, break'll be over anyhow."

"Fuck Salazar."

"Not my type."

"Sit down."

"Well, what damn difference is it gonna make two minutes from now? The point is *I'll* be the the one who has to do it anyway. You ain't gonna do it. Mendez, Piper, Ski, Morales, those guys ain't gonna do it. So . . ." And I just stand there with my knuckles on my belt, trying to look tough, but my trouser seams are wedged up my butt, and in my paper hat, short-sleeve white shirt and red monkey jacket, and knowing that I'm on my way to the soap room so I can clean up a mess that no one else will, I don't feel so tough. Kelly gets the message anyway. He sits there, staring at me with his flat hazel eyes jiggling side to side like they always do when he's twicked. It always makes me sort of nervous. I can't understand how a guy's eyes could do that. Must be some kind of palsy. Then he squints and says, "You noticed how hot it is? It ain't even lunchtime yet and it's just plain damn hot in here."

We're setting up the lunch dishes. In less than an hour we'll be shoveling chow at the junior flyboys and girls. That's what I really hate about this job. That, and cleaning up after them, which pretty much means I hate the whole job. I'm not saying I've got anything against these cadets, not personally. They're smart and polite and everything, but I hate the way the upperclassmen harass the doolies. I hate it when the kids have to stand up at attention right in the middle of a meal and have to spout the chain of command, or the parts of the M-16 rifle. I hate when a bunch of 'em are made to stand up and shout football cheers or wing cheers or flight cheers or squadron cheers. I hate it when you're just getting the ravioli or whatnot to your hundredth flyboy when the first ten are asking for more milk and juice and after you give 'em the milk and the juice, ten people here want more green beans and twenty there want more corn and bread, and there's cheers and chants, and heat and steam and flies and Air Force blue and pink heads everydamnwhere you look, and you're pulling your hot cart alloverthedamnplace and it's big, the size of a VW bus, when you're tired, but then the flybabes split all neat and orderly like, leaving you all this cleaning up to do. All the waste. All the waste. It really gets to me: feed a Boy Scout jamboree with the leftover burgers. Fatten every poor baby on the south side of Colorado Springs with the leftover milk. Ship the green beans, the rice, the macaroni to the shelters all over town and you ain't gotta feel guilty for at least half a week. Abscond with the spuds, fried, baked, au gratin, hashed and browned, boiled, ranched and open up your own damned potato restaurant at zero percent food cost. I mentioned all this to Kelly once and he told me, "Volume buying. Don't cost 'em nothing. And don't give me that trash about starving people and that, 'cause the gover'ment pays for it, and pays your rent, food, clothes and gas, too, and they can do what they please with us *and* the food."

But I can't think about all that now, 'cause I got to hustle buns and get the stuff laid out. Yesterday. 'Cause lunch is just about ready and I know Kelly ain't gonna be much help today since he's steady yakking my ear off about this Barney guy. "Well," he says, "I had duty that very night, anyway, which means I had reveille the next morning and you could bet your sweet ass that little shitbird was getting outta that rack at oh-five-thirty sharp. I knew how to get jarheads up, I tell ya. I'd rap my nightstick on their bedposts, wink the lights, kick over shit cans, and if that didn't work, I'd grab an ankle and pull the guy out. And see, with this Barney kid, I'd not only wake him, but I'd make sure he stayed up by giving him a lawful order to help me get other Marines up."

I said to Kelly, "Say, you want me to get the pitchers laid out or you want to?" Kelly wipes his brow with the inside of his wrist and says, "But when I grabbed his ankle the boy went three kinds of ballistic. Scott, I tell you that not only did this boy take a swing at me, but he pushed over five or six wall lockers and racks. Goddamn things went over like dominoes. . . . You better polish them spoons, lad; they look like hell—and then, see, and then he starts screaming, 'Motherfucker! Motherfucker! I got something for your ass!' And next thing you know he starts punching out windows."

"With his fist?"

"Hell yeah, with his fist. He punches out four before I even know what the hell he's doing. Rattled me pretty bad. That's one of the reasons I retired from the Corps when I did. Crazy hopheads like that, well, you never knew what they were gonna do.

"Well, so this big colored fella, name of Lance Corporal Whitaker, just pushes by me and says, 'Dust,' which I thought was some kind of colored cuss word for white man, but I found out later he meant what they call angel dust, PCP, know what that is?"

He misses my sarcasm when I say, "Tarzan no know. What angel dust?" 'cause he says back, "It's a goddamn drug is what it is. A goddamn drug." He pauses to let this sink in, then says, "So this Lance Corporal Whitaker just walks over to Barney when he's on his seventh or eight window, cutting himself and shedding his blood like he's got an extra couple quarts in his wall locker and don't care, see, and this Whitaker guy just touches Barney on the shoulder and says something like, 'Morning, Barn,' and Barney just stops. Stops dead. I mean he don't move, and neither does anybody else. Everybody's just staring at this kid's bloody hands and arms, and all the blood here and there, in drops and smears. But then this Whitaker fella, just as calm as you please, grabs a towel off Barney's rack, wraps it up and walks Barney to the infirmary. Hey, Scott, we got some bent forks here. Scrounge some good ones, will ya, lad?"

The dining hall is wall-to-wall blue, and Kelly shuts up for a while. But I know he's at sixty degrees 'cause those bones are struggling under his skin like a bag fulla kittens. Things are going smooth and my mind's not even on my work. I'm thinking about taking a long shower, getting into some nonpolyester clothes and calling up Hwasook to make plans for the weekend. Since we're getting paid today the weekend's looking good. We'll go to Deckers, maybe, and she'll take her suntan lotion, a nice bikini and a book, and I'll take my fishing stuff and wine and crackers, cheese, fruit and so forth. Maybe I'll bring a good sci-fi pulp, myself. If the sun cooperates, we'll be fine. As long as we don't run into a bunch of gawking rednecks. Hwasook doesn't understand, but that's why I don't care much for going to the mountains, big, blue-green and beautiful as they are, 'cause of all the RV, truck and motorcycle necks who stare at her like she's some kinda slut and stare at me like they know she wouldn't be as close as a parsec to me if not for my twelve-inch unit and my briefcase fulla heroin.

Hwasook argues that a neck's neck is just as red in town as it is in those hills, and she's got a point, but I have my doubts. Something funny happens to some people when they start huffing pine wood air, drinking beer in the hot sun, eating ash-flavored food. They start feeling like pioneers, mule skinners,

cowboys, desperadoes. To them Hwasook and me start looking like runaway slaves or bloodthirsty savages. They start up
with the yee-haaaaws, and revving their engines, yelling hey
nigger out their windows as they drive by. She doesn't get it,
though, and neither does Kelly. I'm getting twicked off thinking of all this stuff and can't wait till things slow down and he
can get to his point, which I plan to shoot down with all this
stuff I've been thinking about.

Finally, things do slow down, but before I can talk to ol'
Kelly, I spot Mendez coming our way with a hamburger in his
fat mitts. "Hey, Mendez," I say.

"Hey, babe."

"Is it true we're getting paid today?"

Mendez shrugs. "Ask Salazar."

"Fuck Salazar," says Kelly.

"Too skinny," I say, and at the same time Mendez says,
"Nobody's talking to you, Kelly."

Kelly's eyes start to jiggle. "You can kiss my ass, Mendez."

"Wouldn't kiss that wrinkly thing with your *own* lips, old
man." Then he turns back to me. "Look here, bruh, Salazar
needs someone to help Peggy clean up a mess on the east
section."

"He don't have to—"

"It's okay, Kelly, I got it."

And I do get it, leaving Mendez and Kelly to argue with
each other over the rattle and clatter of ninety waiters in monkey suits cleaning up after forty-five hundred cadets, throwing
away probably a quarter ton of food, telling jokes, lies, stories.
I hear Mendez say "racist" at least a half dozen times. I hear
Kelly use the phrase "silver platter." I roll my eyes and keep
walking.

My only problem working next to Peggy is that I'm pretty sure she's got a crush on me. I'm not being conceited or anything, 'cause I'm no stud and Peggy's no fox. She's tall, skinny, forty-five-ish with platinum hair, veiny hands and sky blue, ice blue eyes. She always calls me gorgeous, which I find hard to respond to in a likewise way. She ain't ugly, but I don't like giving her ideas. Right now I'm trying to be polite to her but keep my eyes on the grape juice I'm swabbing up. The flies are having a party. There's a zillion more in her section than there are in Kelly's and mine. "Who's your partner today, Peg?" I ask.

She locks her unbelievably blue eyes on me and smiles at me the same way Mendez smiles at ribs. "Freddy Washington, but I'll trade him for you, gorgeous." I ignore that and ask her where Freddy is. "Salazar's got him in the office, chewing him out for coming in at four-fifty this morning. I'm sure Salazar's having a tougher time than Freddy in there."

I chuckle and say something like Yeah, or, I'll bet, but I notice my hands are trembling and I feel almost sick to my stomach. I'll admit that Peggy usually makes me nervous, but there's something more right now, something I can't get the finger on till two things happen. One: a fly lands on my hand, and I flick it away so hard I drop my mop. Then two: Peggy bends to pick it up for me, and as I bend she looks me square down deep in the eyes. Then I remember.

"So where is Freddy?" I say. Peggy smiles, no doubt thinking she's got me in one of those magic moments where a guy finally notices how beautiful a woman is. "Someone's been working too hard," she says. I shake my head all dramatic like, and say, "I mean, what time did Freddy come in, you say?" I notice her neck is all mottled up red, and I say to myself, Oh

Lord, and I look up at her face and she winks and says, "About five, gorgeous." I wish I could tell her it's not her half-moon beauty, but it does have to do with her, and these flies, and Kelly, and her color and mine, and especially her eyes, the most beautiful thing about her. And now that I really look at her it's got to do with her thin, chapped lips, her hawk nose, her long neck. She reminds me of this girl I thought was my friend for about a semester back in high school. Her name was Dianna Dillman, and she was my lab partner in tenth-grade biology. I never had, like, a crush on Dianna or anything, but I liked her a lot. She was extremely funny, and used to write little notes to me while Mr. Buller was yammering about pond scum, or mitosis, or some such crap. I figure because of Dianna I got Cs instead of Bs in that class, but for almost a whole semester it was worth it. If her little notes didn't crack me up, she'd go for what Buller used to call the "lowbrow" stuff like pretending to get high from breathing the Bunsen burner gas, or just filling her cheeks with air and staring at me for five minutes. Guess you just had to be there. But one day all that stuff just stopped. Dianna acted like I was absent. Bad day, I told myself. So pretty much near the end of bio class, Mr. Buller asked me to stay after. I nudged Dianna with my elbow and whispered to her, "Wonder what this is all about. Nobel Prize, you think?" Dianna didn't say jack. She stared straight ahead and blushed red as her own lipstick.

Turns out the day before, Dianna'd had her wallet lifted from her purse, and since she noticed it missing after bio class, and since I sat right smack next to her at our little black table, she figured I'd snagged it. She never even bothered to ask, just assumed. I didn't take her wallet, and I was glad Buller believed me, but he told me that Dianna didn't wanna be my lab partner anymore. I know Buller would have made her stay at the table if she and I hadn't always been high-timing in class, but I didn't argue. I was pissed. I didn't see her the rest of that day, so I never got the chance to argue my case. And the next day I found a note that she'd slipped into the vents of my locker. I knew it was her, 'cause it was in the same microscopic handwriting of all those funny little notes she'd slip me in class. It went, and I quote, "Only two things in this world that I despise / One of them's niggers / The other one's flies / Only one thing to say about each of these guys / The more I see niggers / The more I like flies."

That was it. Not even a "Love, Dianna."

So this is one more thing to tell Kelly. One thing that's great about being white: The rest of my sophomore year I never could figure out the words to hurt Dianna as much as she'd hurt me. Fact is, I still don't think I could. Six, seven years now, and I still don't think I could.

When I get back Kelly's so hot I'm surprised his little paper hat hasn't burst into flames. "What is it you people want?" he says.

Dominion over nature, time, and the bodies and minds of the white race, I think to myself, but I say, "What'd he say?" and he waves his hairy hands in little circles like he's lost his balance while standing on a log. "Man that guy burns my ass." I don't say nothing. I just start collecting silverware and fighting flies, scraping plates, wiping sweat from my forehead, pulling the seam from the crack of my behind. Hell with these jerks, I say to myself. Hell with spooks, ofays, spicks, gooks, flies, cadets, paychecks, heat, necks, color, links, straight, curls, black, brown, freckles, white. I hate this stuff, I say to myself. I hate all this stuff.

"So," says Kelly, and I'm about two seconds from sticking a fork in his neck. I don't care. I just don't care, but the best thing I can do is let him finish his crap and then blow him away with all this stuff inside me, all this crap I been thinking.

"So," he says, "I figure the guy's crazy and I don't say nothing to him or even look at him when him and Whitaker leave the room. If the United States Marine Corps wants to give welfare to a goddamn lazy hophead that's okay. I'm a short-timer and I don't care. I was in long enough to retire, even though I'd always wanted to do a full twenty-five years. But I just forgot about him. Just went about my business, you see. Least everybody was awake. That was that. I figured I just wouldn't deal with the kid no more.

"But one morning the first sergeant ast a bunch of Marines to redo the squad bay. Seems it was a pretty bad mess. You know it gets like that sometimes. The lads get in a hurry to get to morning chow and miss a spot or two with the swabs and brooms—Will you look at this. Sloppy sons a bitches. Look at this. Some idiot spilled a whole container of milk all over a tray of succotash."

"So fucken what, Kelly, it's not like we're gonna put it in a Tupperware container and stick it in the refrig—"

"So I don't know why I went up there, but for some reason I had to go see somebody in the company office. I don't know, but in order to get to the HQ, you gotta go through the squad bay, see? So I'm going up the stairwell, and I hear all this yelling and cussing, so I run up the rest of the way and Barney's got some little boot private pinned up against the wall. Got his forearm jammed into the kid's windpipe and four other Marines are trying to pull Barney back, but like I told you, Barney's one stout little fella and they're having a pretty tough time getting him to let the little kid loose.

"Well, shit, what was I supposed to do? I help grab Barney's leg. Then his arms, and finally we get him off the kid. This kid's name was Hernandez, Mexican fella, and big old Whitaker was there, and then there was this Samoan fella, Tapua, and another Mexican fella, a guy from Comm Platoon I didn't know, and this white fella name of Grice, a radio tech, I think he was. Looked like the goddamn United Nations, I was thinking. Sure wasn't like the Corps I joined. Not that I got anything against you people being in the service. Just never got used to it."

"Roll me the beverage cart, Kelly," I say, and then I tell him to go ahead. My palms are sweaty, hands trembling. Kelly walks the cart to me and says, "Well, I don't know why we did this. Maybe it was the way Barney relaxed so sudden, the way he just stared out the window like we wasn't even there. Made everybody else relax, too. We all just let him go. And I whispered to Grice to go get the police, and was just getting ready to walk Barney over to the office. I said, 'All right, leatherneck, let's go.' But he just stood there, staring out the window. Then in this real quiet voice he goes, 'I got something for your ass. I got something for all of you.'

"He was at his locker so fast nobody could do nothing. Besides, who the hell knew he'd come back with a pistol? But there he was, waving a silver-plated snub-nose thirty-eight in all our faces. Next thing you know, Hernandez is on his knees, begging for his life. Whitaker's looking sick and pissed off. He sits down on a rack and just starts cussing kinda quiet like, saying how hard he's tried to be a good Marine and how every time he turns around it's some new bullshit. And the Samoan's waving his hands and backing up to the wall, speaking Samoan like he ain't never hearda the United States. The other Mexican kid's just standing there looking white, sweaty and scared. And then there's me. After looking at all these scared young boys I closed my eyes, and lowered my head, see, and it's like I got two brains. One brain's going, Now what the fuck am I supposed to say to this hophead to get him to put the stinking gun down. The other brain's going, I don't give a rolling fuck what he does. I've had it. I've had it. Don't even care anymore—You better get that mop and broom. I'll get these carts."

"We got time, just finish!"

"Well, he shot me."

"I thought you said he *didn't*."

"No, that's not what I said. I just told you I didn't *say* that. Hell yeah he shot me. Right in the thigh, splintered my femur bone like it was rotten bamboo. But the way Hernandez started screaming you'd a thought that Indian bastard'd shot him. But I was the onliest one he shot, and even though Whitaker was on top a Barney before he could get off another round, I knew he was only gonna pump 'em off into me if he'd had the chance."

"So you think he shot you 'cause you're white."

Salazar walks by before Kelly answers and he tells us he'll be passing out the checks at the end of the shift. Kelly glares at

Salazar. At his squeaky, shiny shoes, really. Like he hates 'em. "Man," says Kelly, "I got no respect for that little prick."

"So you think he shot you cause you're white, right?"

He looks at me a real long time, like I'm stupid. I'm not stupid.

"A guy who wears patent leather shoes is too lazy to shine."

"Kelly."

"Huh?"

"Is that your point? What's your point?"

He raises one raven-wing eyebrow. *I* know what he means. *I* get his point. "That's another reason I retired from the Corps. Lotta lazy goddamn boot officers'd wear patent leather 'cause they were just too damn lazy to put a good spit shine on their shoes. Why, do you know that some a them bastards were getting away with wearing patent leather combat boots? Where's the tradition? Where's the pride? Hopheads, shit-birds, AWOLers, rock-n-goddamn roll, hippie-jive-talk a guy can't understand, wash-n-wear uniforms, no-discipline-having, dope-smoking punks—and people, all these people who don't like me . . . for no damn good reason. You think I'd wanna be parta that after twenty-one years? No sir, I don't think so. No thank you.

"Look . . . Look here, I'll swab this time. You sweep, and then let's get outta here. We're getting our pay, Scotty boy."

That's exactly what I did. I swept. I tried to get him to talk more, but he'd just scoot his words around me. I just wanted to talk to him. Talk. But he wouldn't even look me in the eye. It was like sweeping up a four-foot stack of broken dishes. Big pieces with razor-sharp edges, little pieces with needle points, tinier pieces, like little daggers, pieces fine as moon dust. After I finished sweeping, I grabbed my check, went to the locker room, and doffed the monkey suit, slipped into my jeans, sneakers and T-shirt and broke camp. But all the way home I still felt like I was sweeping broken china, from under tables, under chairs, from corners and cracks, and across wide polished floors, military clean and quiet as the mountains.

palm wine

This was fourteen years ago, but it still bothers me as though it happened day before yesterday. I've never talked about this with anyone, and I'm not talking about it now because I expect it to relieve me of painful memory, but because, as they say in Madagascar, the bad is told that the good may appear. So. I was in Senegal on a graduate felowship. I was there to collect and compile West African proverbs. This was to complete my Ph.D. in anthropology, which, I'm afraid, I failed to do. The things I'm going to talk about now had as much to do with that failure as did my laziness, my emotional narrowness and my intellectual mediocrity. I was a good deal younger then, too, but that's no excuse. Not really.

Anyway, one afternoon, instead of collecting proverbs in Yoff village, which I should have done, I went to Dakar with Omar the tailor—a friend of a friend—to buy palm wine. I'd craved palm wine ever since I read Amos Tutuola's novel *The*

Palm-Wine Drinkard in college. Tutuola never attempts to describe the taste, color or smell of palm wine, but because the Drinkard (whose real name is Father of the Gods Who Could Do Anything in This World) can put away 225 kegs of it per day, and because he sojourns through many cruel and horrifying worlds in order to try to retrieve his recently killed palm wine tapster from Deadstown, I figured palm wine had to be pretty good.

As Omar and I boarded the bus, I dreamed palm wine dreams. It must be pale green, I thought, coming from a tree and all. Or milky blue like coconut water. I had it in mind that it must hit the tongue like a dart, and it must make one see the same visions Tutuola himself witnessed. A creature big as a bipedal elephant, sporting two-foot fangs thick as cow's horns; a creature with a million eyes and hundreds of breasts that continuously suckle her young, who swarm her body like maggots; a town where everything and everyone is red as plum flesh; a town where they all walk backwards; a town full of ghosts.

I really had no business going that day. I was at least a month behind in my research because of a lengthy bout with malaria. But I excused myself from work by telling myself that since I had no Wolof proverbs on the subject of drinking, I'd likely encounter a couple that day. But I took my pad, pencils and tape recorder along, knowing I wasn't going to use them.

On the ride to town, I could scarcely pay mind to matters that usually fascinate me. For instance, I would often carefully observe the beggars who board the buses and cry for alms. Their Afro-Arab plaints weave through the bus like serpents, slipping between exquisitely coiffed women and dignified, angular men, wives of the wealthy, daughters of the poor, beardless hustlers, bundled babies, tourists, pickpockets, gendarmes, students. A beautiful plaint could draw coins like salt draws moisture. Some beggars not only sang for indulgence but also sang their thanks. *Jerrejeff, my sister, paradise lies under the feet of mothers. A heart that burns for Allah gives more light than ten thousand suns.* Some of them sang proverbs from the Koran. *Be constant in prayer and give alms. Allah pity him who must beg of a beggar.* Some of them merely cried something very much like "Alms! Alms!" And some of them rasped like reptiles and said little more than "I got only one arm! Gimme money!" and the proverbs they used were usually stale. They were annoying, but even so I often gave them alms, and I recorded them. I guess it was because I liked being in a culture that had a good deal more respect for the poor than my own. And I guess I tried hard to appreciate art forms that were different from the ones I readily understood. But, honestly, as I say, that day I could think of little more than palm wine. It would be cold as winter rain. It would be sweet like berries, and I would drink till my mind went swimming in deep waters.

We alighted the bus in the arrondissement of Fosse, the place Omar insisted was the only place to find the wine. Preoccupied as I was with my palm wine dreams, they weren't enough to keep me from attending Fosse. It's an urban village, a squatter's camp, a smoke-filled bowl of shanties built of rusty corrugated metal, gray splintery planks, cinder block, cement. It smelled of everything: goat skin, pot, green tobacco, fish, overripe fruit, piss, cheap perfume, Gazelle Beer, warm couscous, scorched rice, the sour sharpness of cooking coals. People talked, laughed, sang, cried, argued—the sounds so plangent I felt them in my teeth, my chest, my knees. A woman dressed in blue flowers scolded her teenage son, and the sound lay tart on my tongue. Two boys drummed the bottoms of plastic buckets, while a third played a pop bottle with a stick, and I smelled churai incense. Two little girls danced to the boys' rhythms, their feet invisible with dust, and I felt them on my back.

A beautiful young woman in a paisley wraparound pagne smiled at us, and I rubbed Omar's incipient dreadlocks, his wig of thumbs, as I called them, and said, "Hey, man, there's a wife for you." Omar grinned at me, his amber eyes were crescents, his teeth big as dominoes. "She too old for me, mahn," he said.

"Oh please, brother, she couldn't be older than eighteen."

"Young is better."

"Whatever. Lech."

I didn't really like Omar. He insisted on speaking English with me even though his English was relatively poor. Even when I spoke to him in French or my shaky Wolof he invariably answered me in English. This happened all the time in Senegal and the other francophone countries I traveled. People all around the globe wanted to speak English, and my personal proverb was, Every English-speaking traveler will be a teacher as much as he'll be a student. I suppose if his English had been better I wouldn't have minded, but there were times it led to trouble—like that day—and times when the only thing that bothered me about it was that it was Omar speaking it. Omar the tailor man, always stoned, always grinning, his red-and-amber crescents, his domino teeth, his big olive-shaped head, his wolfish face, his hiccuping laugh jangling every last nerve in my skull. He perpetually thrust his long hands at me for cigarettes, money, favors. "Hey, I and I, you letting me borrow you tape deck?" "Hey, I and I, jokma bene cigarette." He was a self-styled Rastafarian, and he had the notion that since the U.S. and Jamaica are geographically close, Jamaicans and Black Americans were interchangeable. I was pretty certain I was of more value to him as a faux Jamaican than as genuine American.

He was constantly in my face with this "I and I, mahn" stuff, always quoting Peter Tosh couplets, insisting I put them in my book. (I could never get him to understand the nature of my work.) Moreover, it took him six months to sew one lousy pair of pants and one lousy shirt for me, items I was dumb enough to pay him in advance for. From the day he measured me to the day I actually donned the clothes I'd lost twenty-six pounds. (Constant diarrhea and a fish-and-rice diet will do that to you.) But I wasn't about to ask him to take them in, though. I only had a year's worth of fellowship money, after all.

Omar always spoke of his great volume of work, his busy-ness, the tremendous pressure he was under, but each and every time I made it to his shop to pick up my outfit, I'd find him sitting with four or five friends, twisting his locks, putting the buzz on, yakking it up. "Hey, I and I, come in! I don't see you a long time."

In northern Africa they say, Bear him unlucky, don't bear him lazy. But I bore Omar because he was a friend of my good friend and assistant Idrissa, who, at the time, was visiting his girlfriend in Paris. I went with Omar to get the palm wine because Omar, who knew Fosse a great deal better than Idrissa did, insisted that day was the only time in palm wine season he would be able to make the trip. He told me that Idrissa wouldn't be back till the season was well over. Originally, the three of us were to have made the trip, but Idrissa's girlfriend sent him an erotic letter and a ticket to Paris. And money. We blinked; Idrissa was gone, and since Omar was so "pressed for time," we wasted none of it getting to the city. As I walked the ghetto with Omar I reflected on how Idrissa would often fill things in for me with his extemporaneous discussions of the history, economics and myths about wherever in Senegal we happened to be. Idrissa was self-educated and garrulous. My kind of person. He was also very proud of his Senegalese heritage. He seemed to know everything about the country. As Omar and I walked, I told myself that if Idrissa had been there, I would have been learning things. What did I know?

On our walk, Omar seldom spoke. He seemed unable to answer any of my questions about the place, so after about ten minutes I stopped asking. We walked what seemed to me the entire ghetto, and must have inquired at about eight or nine places without seeing a drop of palm wine. Each inquiry involved the usual African procedure—shake hands all around, ask about each other's friends, families, health, work; ask for the wine, learn they have none, ask them who might, shake hands, leave. It was getting close to dusk now, and our long shadows undulated before us over the packed soil. I was getting a little hungry, and I kept eyeing the street vendors who braised brochettes of mutton along the curb of the main street. The white smoke rose up and plumed into the streets, raining barbecue smells everywhere. I said, "Looks like we're not getting the wine today. Tell you what, why don't we—"

"Is not the season-quoi," Omar said as we rambled into a small, secluded yard. It was surrounded by several tin-roofed houses, some with blanket doors, insides lighted mostly by kerosene or candles. Here and there, though, I could see that some places had electricity. Omar crossed his arms as we drew to a stop. "We stay this place and two more," he said, "then I and I go."

"Aye-aye," I said.

Four young men sat on a dusty porch passing a cigarette among themselves. Several toddlers, each runny-nosed and ashy-kneed, frenetically crisscrossed in front of the men, pretending to grab for the cigarette. Until they saw me. Then they stopped and one of the older ones approached us, reached out a hand and said, "Toubobie, mawney." Omar said, in Wolof, "This man isn't a toubob. This is a black man. An American brother." I answered in Wolof, too. "Give me a proverb and I'll give you money." The boy ran away grinning, and the men laughed. I drew my cigarettes from my shirt pocket, tapped out eight and gave two to each man.

"Where's Doudou?" Omar asked the men.

They told him Doudou, whoever he was, had left a half hour before, but was expected back very soon. One of the men, a short, muscular man in a T-shirt and a pair of those voluminous trousers called chayas, detached himself from his friends, and walked into one of the houses. He returned, carrying a small green liquor bottle. I felt my eyebrows arch. The stuff itself, I was thinking. I imagined myself getting pied with these boys, so drunk I'm hugging them, telling them I love them, and goddamn it where's old Doudou? I miss that bastid. The man in the chayas unscrewed the lid with sacremental delicacy, drank and passed the bottle on. I watched the men's faces go soft when each passed the bottle on to his brother. I took the bottle rather more aggressively than was polite, and I apologized to the man who'd handed it to me. Omar winked at me. "You don't know what bottle is-quoi?" Omar had the irritating habit of using the tag "quoi" after most of his sentences.

He did it in English, French, Wolof, and his own language, Bambara. It wasn't an uncommon habit in French West Africa, but Omar wore it down to a nub.

"Paaalm wiiine," I said in a low, throaty voice the way you'd say an old love's name. My God, what was wrong with me? I was behaving as though, like the Drinkard himself, I had fought the beast with the lethal gaze and shovel-sized scales, or had spent the night in the bagful of creatures with ice cold, sandpapery hair, that I'd done some heroic thing, and the stuff in the green bottle was my reward. As I brought the bottle to my lips, Omar said, "It's no palm wine, I and I." I drank before Omar's words even registered, and the liquid burned to my navel. It was very much like a strong tequila. No, that's an understatement. If this drink and tequila went to prison, this drink would make tequila its cabin boy. "Is much stronger than palm wine," said Omar.

My throat had closed up and it took me a few seconds before I could speak. All I could manage was to hiss, "Jeeezuz!" And abruptly one of the young men, a Franco-Senegalese with golden hair and green eyes said, "Jeeezuz," but then he continued in rapid Wolof and I lost him. Soon, all five of them were laughing, saying "Jeeezuz, Jeezuz," working the joke, extending it, jerking it around like taffy. My blood rose to my skin, and every muscle in my back knotted. I squinted at Omar, who looked back at me with eyes both reassuring and provocative, and he said, "He saying he like Americaine noire talk. You know, you say-quoi, 'Jeeezuz,' and 'Sheeee,' and 'Maaaaan-quoi.' We like the Americaine noire talk." His mouth hovered this close to a smirk.

I was furious, but I had no choice but to grin and play along. I lit a smoke and said Jeezuz and Jeezuz Christ, and

Jeezuz H. Christ, "cuttin' the monkey," as my dad would put it. My stomach felt as though it were full of mosquitoes. My hands trembled. I wanted to kick Omar's face in. His hiccupping giggles rose above the sound of everyone else's laughter, and his body jerked about convulsively. Yeah, choke on it, I thought. But I didn't have to endure the humiliation long, for soon an extremely tall, very black, very big-boned man joined us, and Omar said, "Doudou!" and fiercely shook hands with the giant. Doudou nodded my way and said, in Wolof, "What's this thing?" and I froze with astonishment. Thing? I tried to interpret Omar's lengthy explanation, but his back was to me and he was speaking very rapidly. As I say, my Wolof was never very good. Doudou placed his hands on his hips and squinted at the ground as though he'd lost something very small. The big man nodded now and then. Then he looked at me, and said in French, "It's late in the season, but I know where there's lots of palm wine." He immediately wheeled about and began striding away. Omar followed, then I.

The walk was longer than I'd expected, and by the time we got to the place, the deep blue twilight had completely absorbed our shadows. After seven or eight months of living in Senegal, I had become used to following strangers into unfamiliar places in the night. But even so, I felt uneasy. I watched the night as a sentry would, trying to note every movement and sound. There was nothing extraordinary about the things I saw on the way, but even today they remain vivid as if I'd seen them the day before yesterday—a three-year-old girl in a faded pink dress, sitting on a porch; a cat-sized rat sitting atop an overflowing garbage crate; a man in a yellow shirt and blue tie talking to a bald man wearing a maroon khaftan; a half moon made half again by a knot of scaly clouds; Omar's wig of thumbs; Doudou's broad back. I wasn't thinking much about palm wine.

It was an inconspicuous place, built from the same stuff, built in the same way practically every other place in Fosse was. Perhaps a half dozen candles lit the room, but rather than clarify they muddied the darkness. I couldn't tell whether there were six other men in the place or twelve. I couldn't make out the proprietress's face or anything about her, for that matter. The only unchanging features were her eyes, an unnatural olive black and egg white, large, perpetually doleful. But was her expression stern or soft? As the candlelight shifted, heaved, bent, so did her shape and demeanor. At times she seemed big as Doudou, and at other times she seemed only five foot two or so. One moment she looked fifty; a second later, twenty-three. Her dress was sometimes blue, sometimes mauve. I couldn't stop staring at her, and I couldn't stop imagining that the light in the room was incrementally being siphoned away, and that my skull was being squeezed as if in the crook of a great headlocking arm, and that the woman swelled to two, three, four times her size, and split her dress like ripe fruit skin, and glowed naked, eggplant black like a burnished goddess, and that she stared at me with those unchanging olive and egg eyes. It's that stuff I drank, I kept saying to myself. It's that stuff they gave me. Then with increasing clarity I heard a hiss as though air were rushing from my very own ears, and the sound grew louder, so loud the air itself seemed to be torn in half like a long curtain, until it abruptly stopped with the sound of a cork being popped from a bottle; then everything was normal again, and I looked around the room half embarrassed as if the ridiculous things in my head had been projected on the wall before me for all to see, and I saw that Doudou was staring at me with a look of bemused deprecation. I felt myself blush. I smiled rather stupidly at the giant, and he cocked his head just a touch to the left, but made no change in his facial expression. I quickly looked back at the woman.

She told my associates that the wine was still quite fresh, and she swung her arm with a graceful backhand motion before ten plastic gallon jugs apparently full to the neck with the wine. It was very cheap, she said. Then she dipped her hands into a large plastic pan of water on the table that stood between herself and us. She did it the way a surgeon might wash her hands, scooping the water, letting it run to the elbows. In the same water she washed two bottles and laid them aside. Next, she poured a little palm wine into a tumbler, walked to the door, then poured the contents on the ground outside. I could feel excitement sparking up again in my stomach. "Is ritual," said Omar, but when I asked him what it meant, he ignored me.

The woman returned to the jug, filled the bottom half inch of her tumbler with wine and took two perfunctory sips. After that she slipped a screened funnel into the first bottle's neck, filled the bottle, then filled the second bottle in the same way. Omar lifted one of the bottles, took a whiff then a sip. I closely watched his face, but his expression told me little. He arched both eyebrows and nodded a bit. The woman handed the second bottle to Doudou, and he did pretty much what Omar had. I don't recall noting his expression. Then Omar handed me his bottle.

It was awful. It was *awful*. It was awful. Though Idrissa had warned me about the taste, I had had the impression that he was trying to prepare me for the fact that it doesn't taste like conventional wines. I was prepared for many things, a musky flavor, a fruity flavor, dryness, tartness, even blandness. But for me, the only really pleasant aspect of the liquid was its color, cloudy white like a liquid pine cleaner mixed with water. It had a slightly alcoholic tang and smelled sulfuric. It had a distinctly sour bouquet which reminded me of something I very much hated as a kid. If you could make wine from egg salad and vinegar, palm wine is pretty much what you'd get.

Really, the stuff was impossible to drink, but I did my best. The ordeal might have gone more easily had Omar not been Omar—singing reggae music off-key, slapping my back, philosophizing in a language he didn't understand, toasting a unified Africa, then toasting the mighty Rastafari, toasting me, then Doudou. But the thing that made the ordeal in the bar most unpleasant was that Doudou glared at me for what felt like ten unbroken minutes. He stared at my profile as though my face were his property. I couldn't bring myself to confront him. He was just so fucking huge. He was not merely tall—perhaps six foot eight? or so—but his bones were pillars, his face a broad iron shield. He gave off heat, he bowed the very atmosphere of the room. Wasn't it enough I had to drink that swill? Did I need the additional burden of drinking from under the millstone of this man's glare? Just as I was about to slam my bottle to the table and stalk out, Doudou said, in French, "An American."

"Americano," I said.

"Amerikanski," he said.

"That's right. We've got that pretty much nailed down."

"Hey," Omar said, "you like the palm wine?"

Before I could answer, Doudou said, "He doesn't like the wine, Omar."

"Who says I don't?"

Doudou cocked an eyebrow, and looked at the low-burning candle on our table. He rolled the bottle between his fingers as if it were pencil thin. "I tell you he doesn't like it, Omar." Then he looked at me, and said, "*I* say you don't." I felt cold everywhere. A small, painful knot hardened between my shoulder blades, as so often happens when I'm angry.

"You know," I said, stretching my back, rolling my shoulders, "I'm not going to argue about something so trivial." Then I turned to Omar, and said in English, "Omar, the wine is very good. Excellent."

Omar shrugged, and said, "Is okay, I think. Little old."

We were silent after that, and Doudou stopped staring, but it got no more comfortable. Two men started to argue politics, something about the increasing prices of rice and millet, something about Islamic law, and when it got to the table-banging stage, Omar suggested we leave. I had suffered through two glasses of this liquid acquired taste, and Omar, much to my regret, bought me two liters of the wine to take home. But I did want to go home, and said so. But Doudou said, "You must stay for tea." Omar said yes before I could say no, and I knew it would be impolite to leave without Omar. We walked back to Doudou's place and I saw that the young men were still quietly getting happy on the Senegalese tequila. Doudou sat in a chair on the porch and sent the young man in chayas into the house and he returned with a boom box and a handful of tapes. He threw in a Crusaders tape, and immediately two of the men began to complain. They wanted Senegalese music, but Doudou calmly raised his hand and pointed to me. The men fell silent, and I said, "I don't have to have American music."

"Sure you do," said the big man. He leaned so far back in his chair that its front legs were ten inches off the porch, and the back of the chair rested against the windowsill. His feet stayed flat on the ground.

"Your French is good," I said.

"Better than yours," he said. He was smiling, and I couldn't see a shred of contempt in his expression, but that burned up the last of my calm. It was full dark, but I could see his broad smooth face clearly, for the house's light illuminated it. It hung before the window like a paper lantern, like a planet. Looking back on it, I can see that I must have offended him. He must have thought I was evincing surprise that he, a denizen of Fosse, could speak as well as he did. Actually I was just trying to make conversation. When the bottle came my way I tipped it and drank a full inch of it. "Thanks for the hospitality," I said. Doudou folded his arms, and tipped his head forward, removing it from the light. "Amerikanski," he said. One of the men chuckled.

Omar sat "Indian" style a foot to my right. He rolled a very large spliff from about a half ounce of pot and an eight-by-ten-inch square of newspaper. He handed it to the man sitting across from him, the Franco-Senegalese with the golden hair. The comedian. "Where's the tea?" the man asked in Wolof. "Eh?" said Doudou, and then he pointed to the boom box. The man in the chayas turned it down. The golden-haired man repeated his question. Doudou's only reply was, "Ismaila, get the tea," and the young man in the chayas rose once again, and came back quickly with the Primus stove, the glasses, the sugar and the tea.

"Omar tells me that you're an anthropologist," said Doudou.

"That's right," I said.

"The study of primitive cultures." Doudou said this as though he'd read these words off the back of a bottle. A dangerous sort of neutrality, as I saw it. It grew so still for a moment there, that I jumped when Ismaila lit the stove; the gas had burst into blue flame with a sudden *woof* and I found myself glaring at Ismaila as though he'd betrayed me. I cleared my throat, said, "That's only one aspect of anthropology . . ." I struggled for words. When I'm nervous I can barely speak my own language, let alone another's, but I managed to say, ". . . but I to study the living cultures." There, I thought, that was nice. I went on to explain that the discipline of anthropology was changing all the time, that it had less to do with so-called primitive cultures and more to do with the study of the phenomenon of culture and the many ways it can be expressed. The light from the stove's flame cast ghost light over the four of us who sat around it. One of the men, a short man with batlike ears, sat behind me and Omar. He was in silhouette as was Doudou, up there on the porch. The man with the strange ears tapped my shoulder and handed me the spliff. I took a perfunctory hit, and handed it to Omar. "Ganjaaaa," said Omar.

"I knew an anthropologist once," said Doudou, "who told me I should be proud to be part of such a noble, ancient and primitive people." He paused long enough for me to actually hear the water begin to boil. Then he said, "What aspect of anthropology do you think he studied?"

"Couldn't tell you," I said.

"Too bad."

"Maybe," I said, "he trying to tell you that primitive . . . I mean, that in this case 'primitive' mean the same thing as 'pure.'"

"Really. 'In this case,' you say."

"I can only—"

"Was I supposed to have been offended by his language? Are you saying we Africans should be offended by words like 'primitive'?" He placed his great hands on his knees, sat up straight. It occurred to me he was trying to look regal. It worked. I could feel myself tremulously unscrewing the top of one of my palm wine bottles, and I took a nip from it. My sinuses filled with its sour bouquet. "Well . . . you sounded offended," I said.

"Who studies your people?"

"What?"

"Do you have anthropologists milling about your neighborhood? Do they write down everything you say?"

"Look, I know how you must—"

Doudou turned away from me. "Ismaila, how's the tea coming?" he said.

"No problems," said Ismaila.

"Look here," I said, but before I could continue, the man with the pointed ears said, "I get offended. I get very offended. You write us down. You don't respect us. You come here and steal from us. It's a very bad thing, and you, you should know better."

"What, because I'm black?"

"Black," said Doudou, with a chuckle.

"Is fine, I and I. Is very nice."

"What the fuck's that supposed to mean, Omar?" I said. "Look, I'm trying to help all black people by recovering our forgot things."

"Your 'lost' things," Ismaila said quietly as he dumped two or three handfuls of tea into the boiling water. He removed the pot from the flame and let it steep for a few minutes. One of the men, a bald, chubby man with a single thick eyebrow, rose from the ground and began fiddling with the boom box. He put in a tape by some Senegalese group, and turned it up a bit. The guitar sounded like crystal bells, the base like a springy heartbeat; the singer's nasal voice wound like a tendril around the rhythm. As Ismaila sang with the tape, he split the contents of the pot between two large glasses, filling each about halfway, and dumped three heaps of sugar into each glass. While he worked, I kept nipping at the palm wine like a man who can't stop nipping at the pinky nail of his right hand even though he's down to the bloody quick. The more I drank, the odder its flavors seemed to me. It was liquid egg, ammonia, spoiled fish, wet leather, piss. The taste wouldn't hold still, and soon enough it wholly faded. The roof of my mouth, my sinuses, my temples began to throb with a mild achiness, and if I'd had food in my belly that evening, I might have chucked it up. Ismaila began tossing the contents of the glasses from one glass to the other. I could see that Omar was following his movements with great intent.

"What's all this about, Omar?" I said in English. "Why are these guys fucking with me?" I hoped he'd understood me, and I hoped that none of his friends would suddenly reveal himself as a fluent speaker of English. I also ended up wishing Idrissa were there when Omar said, "No worry, I and I; the tea is good."

"Things lost?" said Doudou. "That must mean you're not pure-quoi, that you think you can come here and bathe in our primitive dye."

Omar and I exchanged looks, our heads turning simultane-

81

ously. I was encouraged by that speck of consanguinity. It emboldened me. "Want some palm wine?" I said to Doudou. "It really tastes like crap."

The giant shifted slightly in his chair. He said nothing for maybe fifteen seconds. "How does it feel," he said, "to be a black toubob?" I felt my face suddenly grow hot. My guts felt as if they were in a slow meltdown. I took a large draft of the wine and disgust made me wince. "By 'toubob,' " I asked, "do you mean 'stranger' or 'white'? I understand it can be used both ways."

Doudou leaned forward in the chair and it snapped and popped as if it were on fire. It appeared for a moment he was going to rise from his chair, and everything in me tightened, screwed down, clamped, but he merely leaned and said, "In Wolof, 'toubob' is 'toubob' is 'toubob.' " The blood beat so hard beneath my skin, I couldn't hear the music for a few seconds. I tried to breathe deeply, but I couldn't. All I could do was drink that foul wine and quiver with anger. I stared for a long time at some pinprick point in the air between me and Doudou. It was as though the world or I had collapsed into that tiny point of blackness, which, after I don't know how long, opened like a sleepy eye, and I realized that I'd been watching Ismaila hand around small glasses of tea. First to Omar, then to Doudou, then to the golden-haired man, then to the man with the bat ears, then to the chubby bald man with the unibrow. Ismaila didn't even look my way. I sat there with blood beating my temples. Their tea-sipping sounded like sheets tearing.

Then Ismaila brewed a second round of tea, but I received no tea in that round either. When everyone finished, Ismaila simply turned off the stove and began gathering the cups and

things. It was the most extraordinary breach of Senegalese eti-
quette I'd seen in the year I lived there. No one, not even
Omar, said a word. Omar, for his part, looked altogether grim.
He leaned toward me and whispered, "You got no tea, huh?" I
could hear the nervous tremor in his voice.

"It's no big deal, Omar."

"I and I, you tell him for give you the tea-quoi."

"Skip it."

"Quoi?"

"Forget about the tea. I got this." I raised the bottle, and
finished it.

"He *must* give you the tea."

"Omar, that big motherfucker don't have to 'must' shit."

Omar relit the spliff and said, "Is bad, mahn, is very bad."
He offered me the spliff, but I waved if off and opened up my
second bottle. Omar often displayed what one could call dis-
placement behavior when he didn't understand me. He'd
swiftly change the subject, or say something noncommital. You
might think that this was one more thing that bothered me
about him, but actually I found it rather endearing, for some
reason. "Is bad, I and I. He do bad."

"Fuck it."

The other men had moved closer to the big man. Two sat
on the ground; two squatted on the porch. They spoke quietly,
but every so often they burst forth with laughter. I drank
and stared at the bottle. "Listen in you ears, I and I," said
Omar. "You must strong Doudou. You must put him and
strong him."

"Speak French, Omar."

"No, no. You must. He do this now and every day-quoi.
Every day. Only if you strong him he can't do it."

I took this to mean that unless I "stronged" Doudou he would treat me badly every time he saw me, but I wasn't figuring on seeing him again and I whispered as much to Omar—in French, so there'd be no mistake. "And besides," I said, "as your countrymen say, 'The man who wants to blow out his own brains needs not fear their being blown out by others.' " I raised the bottle, but couldn't bring myself to drink from it this once.

"No, mahn, strong him. He do this and then 'nother man, then 'nother, then 'nother man. All the time. All day."

"Sheeit, how on earth could—"

"Believe in me, I and I—"

". . . anything to do with how other people treat me, man. Let's get out of here. I can't just—"

Omar clutched my knee so firmly I understood—or thought I did—the depth of his conviction. "You make him strong on him now, and it will be fine for you." Then he removed his hand from my knee and touched it to his chest and said, "For me, too." It was then that I realized that the incident with the tea was meant for Omar as much as for me. Omar had brought me as an honored guest, or as a conversation piece, or as his chance to show his friends just how good his English was. But why was it up to me, either as symbol or as a genuine friend, to recover his lustre? I was the guest, right? I told myself to just sit there, and drink, then leave. But suddenly, the men around Doudou burst into laughter again, and I distinctly heard the golden-haired comedian say, "Jeeezuuuz!" and I felt my body rising stiff from the ground in jerky motions. I walked straight up to Doudou, dropped my half-empty bottle at his feet and slugged him so hard I'm certain I broke his nose. I know for certain I broke my finger.

Doudou went tumbling from his chair and landed facedown on the porch. He struggled to get up, but fell forward, his head rolling side to side. His blood looked like black coins there on the porch. All the men rushed up to him, excepting the chubby man, who shoved me off the porch. I went down on my ass, but sprung up almost immediately. I was still pugnacious, but in a very small, very stupid way. Omar removed his shirt and pressed it to Doudou's nose.

I said, "Is he okay?"

No one replied.

I said, "We can get him a cab, get him to a doctor. I'll pay for the cab; I'll pay the doctor." And someone told me in Wolof that I could go out and fuck a relative. I stepped closer to the lot of them, out of shame and concern rather than anger, but Omar handed his shirt to Ismaila, stepped toward me with his palm leveled at my chest. "You go now," he said.

"But I thought you said—"

"You are not a good man." He turned back toward Doudou, whom they'd moved to the chair. The man with the strange ears left with a plastic bucket to retrieve fresh water. They all had their backs to me. I stood there a good long while, sick to my stomach from palm wine or shame, or both. After some minutes, Omar turned toward me for the briefest moment, and said, "Don't come again, Bertrand." He said this in French.

I left the little courtyard, and immediately lost my way. I wandered Fosse for what must have been ten years. On my way, I encountered an army of headless men who chased me with machetes. Blood gushed from their necks like geysers. Later, I was eaten and regurgitated by a creature with three thousand sharp fangs in its big red mouth. It had the head of a lion, and its long snaky body bristled with forty-four powerful baboon arms. Months later in this strange new world, I discovered a town where everyone ate glass, rocks, wood, dirt, bugs, etc., but grew sick at the sight and smell of vegetables, rice, couscous, fish. They captured me and tried to make me eat sand, but I brandished a yam I'd had in my pocket and when they all fell ill at the sight of it, I ran away. In another town I met a man who was handsome and elegant in every way, and I followed him to his home simply to jealously gaze at him. But while on the way to his own home, I saw him stop at other people's homes, and at every place he stopped, he'd remove part of his body and return it to the person from whom he'd borrowed it. At each place he'd leave a leg, or an arm, or a hand, and so forth, so by the time he got home, I discovered he was but a skull, who rolled across the ground like a common stone. It made me sad to see his beauty vanish so, and I walked all the way back to my home in Denver with my shoulders rounded and my head bent low. And when my people asked me what I found on my long long journey, I told them, "Palm wine. But it wasn't in season, so I have nothing to give you."

boot

i

No, that's not what I'm saying. I'm not saying it's okay to lie. All I'm saying, Coburn, is—if you'll let me—is that there're lies you believe in, and lies you don't believe in. This is a lie I believed in, and it took me a long time to shake it off.

I think it was the punishment that made it so hard. I mean, look, they made you haul around sixteen-pound hammers everywhere you went. You had to carry these things around like they were your M-16s. Spent *eight* hours a day making cement blocks into powder with those hammers, dude. I'm telling you. You were fucking chained together at the ankle with at least forty other recruits, brother. You're damn right they did. And hot? Let me tell you, Coburn, when you get to thinking that packing bags and humping groceries at our little Safeway is a burden, just think about old Bones here chained like a bald-headed slave to other slaves in ninety-by-ninety weather. Think about this poor bastard breathing hot white dust for eight hours a day while he's wrestling a sixteen-pound hammer to the sound of his keeper's whistle. One blast for up, one for down.

You're damn right it's hard, but the rest of it was hard, too. In the Corrective Custody Platoon they had this problem: they had to make it harder than regular boot camp, but not actually kill people. In regular boot camp they make you run, march, polish shit, climb obstacle courses and so forth. You take courses in rifle maintenance, first aid, close combat, swimming. None of it's fun, but it's never boring, especially when they punish your ass. Mostly it's push-ups and squat-thrusts, which you do for the slightest infractions.

Say you fold your towel wrong, say you're talking in formation, say you look your drill instructor in the eye, say you refer to yourself as "I" instead of "the private," say you refer to your DI as "you," rather than "Drill Instructor, Staff Sergeant So-and-so," say you're caught cussing under your breath while the DI is picking on some dumb little recruit you feel sorry for, or you move too slow when you're called, or you roll your eyes when your Drill Instructor barks at you, or you wipe sweat out your eyes, or swat a bug when you're supposed to be at attention. Say you're ugly and the DI just can't stand the sight of you. These are the times the DI will put you on your face. And they don't just do you till you break into a little sweat and get a touch winded. Nope, they do you till the floor is slick with your sweat, till your muscles tremble like you got the flu. I seen some guys cry. Swear to God.

I remember one time the DI was bending and thrusting us in this sandpit outside our squad bay. This one guy spits a loogie onto the sand, like a guy'll do when he's overworked. Well, the DI says, "Say, Boot, whachu doing spitting on my nice clean deck. You pick that goop up and put it back where you found it." And the guy did, sand and all.

So this is typical boot camp stuff. It won't kill you, and neither will CCP, but it does make regular boot camp look like sex with your fantasy girlfriend. It lasts for one week, CCP, if you're lucky—two or three if you really don't get it the first time. But an hour in that place will change you fast. Make you feel wronged by the man, make you feel like your lie wasn't a lie 'cause it was all so hard. And even though they keep you busy for sixteen hours a day, like they do in regular bootsville, it feels like you got more time to think. I guess it's the monotony, the one-track rhythm of the system. You spend one-third of the day collecting dust and pain in every pore of your body. You spend another third washing the dust out your clothes, eating, shining your white boots back into black glass. You shine your brass, reblock your cover, which before the end of the day, the DIs have knocked off your head at least a half dozen times, and forty guys have tromped on. They put you on your face for so much as blinking without permission, but it's all so quiet-like, except for the whistle.

In regular bootsville, when they put you on your face, you hear this sound, like the air sort of crackling. Everybody's—you know—angry. There's a sound to it, like florescent lights in a gym. But in CCP, it's quiet—everybody's bummed, everybody's thinking about what they didn't do wrong. You feel used, and used up.

The last third of the day's supposed to be about rest, and it pretty much is, for regular boot camp, but in Corrective Custody, you don't hear the crackling sound until the lights are out and everybody's in the rack. Then, it's like everybody's in bed eating walnuts, it's so loud with anger. Punishment makes you think about shit, but it doesn't make you see the light. No sir. All night long you're knotted up in blind anger, your sheets twisted round your neck, your fists still hard enough to grip the hammer.

I know you, Coburn, you're one of them romantic dudes who think prison would be like some movie where the hero gets real mad while breaking a rock and he just starts flailing away at it. Then we're supposed to know that the hero's pretending the rock is the head of the evil guard, or the reptile-heart motherjump who turned him in, or some such nonsense.

Well, as a matter of fact, that's not true. When you're actually busting rocks, you're pretty much busting rocks. You're too tired to dabble in imagination. Your brain shuts off, your body goes robot on you. All you can see is your rock, and your boot, a sixteen-pound blur and white dust. It's in that last third of the day when you think about how that piece of concrete you're working on is Captain Hoeg's head, or Drill Instructor Allen's head, or that weaselly bucktoothed-ass Private Grice's head, but mostly what you think about is what you did to get yourself there. For me, it was what I thought was the truth. I swear to you, young blood, the more I twisted in those sheets, the more I believed I hadn't lied.

What? No thanks, man, I'm not doing meat these days.

No, it's nothing moral. It's just I've spent over seven thousand hours of my life cutting up meat, and I'm sick of looking at it. If it was a moral thing, I couldn't do the job. Besides, how could I give up these nifty little paper hats?

I will have a taste of that pie there, though.

Well, it's okaaay. A little stale, maybe.

Well, lemme get back to my story.

When Drill Instructor Staff Sergeant Allen asked me to

cheat on the firing line, I said, "Sir-yes-sir; aye-aye-sir." I'm sure you've heard military talk before. You've seen those movies. The first and last words outta your mouth are supposed to be "sir." What they don't say in the movies, though, like I said before, is you can't use personal pronouns like "you," or "me," or "I." If you say, like, "I feel sick," instead of "The private feels sick," the DI'll put his face as close to yours as the brim of his campaign cover'll let him, and this prick'll say something to you like, "Eye? Eye? You got something in yo I, Prive?" And so like you say, "You don't understand. I'm really sick."

"Ewe? Ewe? Do I look like a sheep to you, boy? Do you wanna fuck me, Private?" And he'll start peckin at your forehead, or your ear with the edge of his campaign cover, like his name's Woody Wood, Jr. and your name's Bob Sycamore. No man has ever got in your face like that, and stunk like that and yelled like that, and didn't move away without a fat lip, but you are scared. For one thing, DIs wear about a quart of bad cologne every day, and some of them chew tobacco, so as to work this subliminal crap on your head. The heavy smell overwhelms you, but you believe it's the DI. For another thing, you know they can have your narrow ass arrested if you so much as raise your hand to them. For another thing, the military scrubs brains smooth in boot camp.

But like I'm saying, this DI'll say, he'll say, "Are-you-tryin-to-piss-me-off-to-day-Maggot? Are you trying to put me on the rag, today?" By this time, you're so angry and worked up, you wanna bite his nose off, but you won't move, 'cause you're too angry, and too scared. You're afraid you'll kill everybody, and you won't stop killing till you've left a bloodred ribbon around the whole stinking globe. Naw, I don't think so, Coburn, not even a badass like you would move. And then he'll point to the ground and say, "Get down on my deck and give me fi'ty bend-and-thrust, Bitch." And it's a good thing he does, too, 'cause it helps you work off the rage.

Well no, Staff Sergeant Allen didn't actually say "cheat" but that's what he was asking me. I knew that right away. I mean all this bullshit about, "Ah, well, Private Hay-riss, I cain't give you a lawful order to do this, but some of our privates are injuring our platoon average on the range here." Fucking gorilla was as nice as could be, which told me everything I needed to know. Even put his hand on my shoulder, like his name was Jimmy J. Coach or something. I mean, please, the guy hated me. It killed him I was his best shooter, and it killed him there were so many assback shooters in his platoon that season.

But it's not like what we did was original. I was told a couple years later that DIs pretty much always use ringers on the firing line to raise their platoon marksmanship averages. The higher the average, the more easy the guy gets promoted. Everybody does it.

But there he was, *asking* me—hell, considering how he felt about me, and considering this was Marine Corps basic training, he was practically on his knees, kissing my smoothies. Yeah, he dropped his big old fuzzy mitt on my shoulder, scrunched up those big-assed hedgehog eyebrows all serious-like, and gets all confidential in my face. It freaked me out, him getting so close to me like that without him yelling. He had a jaw like half a watermelon, and it always looked like he needed a shave—you know, with that blue-green look to it? His eyes had these big droopy Robert Mitchum lids. And his teeth were splayed and bucked, like some kind of cartoon ogre. He had that whole fear-o'-God-in-you stuff screwed down tight partly because he was so ugly. It shoulda been a hick face, one of them faces that said, Hey, I'm the biggest slack-jawed, no-intellect-having, proto-sea-urchin-brain-having, shoe-drooling, motherless lizard that ever put feet to dirt.

But, no, it wasn't quite that kind of face. No, this guy had some of the blackest, coldest eyes I'd ever seen in my life. And they were smart eyes. Eyes that kinda went, I know that you know that I know that you know.

Hey, I won't lie to you, by the time we were in the rifle range phase of boot camp—about six weeks in?—I was afraid of him. Of course, you're supposed to be afraid of DIs or the whole damned thing wouldn't work. You fear the DI, you fear looking like a puss in front of the other boots, you fear shaming your family. You fear going to jail. It's that fear that keeps seventy-five recruits with loaded M-16s from shooting their drill instructors to fucking rags. But like I tell you, DIs play so many mind games with you in the first phase of boot camp that you'd shoot your little sister before you'd shoot one of them puppies.

From the very first night of basic training, they make you hurry everywhere, but you stand in formations and lines, waiting for nothing for hours at a time. If you talk or move without permission in that line, they put you on your face. They cut all your hair off in less than a minute, just as soon as you get off the bus. I mean, straight from the bus, right to the barber shop. (I know that don't mean nothing to you nineties boys, with all that skinhead shit you do, but in the seventies it shocked the pants off you.) They make you strip, shower and shave. They make you pack all your civilian trash in boxes and address it to your parents. They bark at you constantly, in this guttural language you can't understand any better'n you can understand a seal.

Hell yes it works. It's worked for over two hundred years or better, in this country. In the first few days, they keep you tired, never let you get quite enough sleep, or get quite enough to eat, so you're always just a little off balance, and your mind's empty. And, man, they keep at you. I once saw three drill instructors standing around this one recruit on the third-floor squad bay balcony?

What? Oh, well the Marines stopped using the old Quonset huts back in the late sixties, pretty much, and started housing recruits and others in these buildings that looked like big pastel motel complexes. Three stories high, with a small balcony for the DIs to use. Well, anyhow, this guy I'm telling you about? They had him in one of those deals where if you agree with one DI, you're calling the other one a liar. They were pros at this one. Did it every chance they got. It'd make your head do three-sixties. Well, this poor boot's mind popped and he jumped off the balcony. So, the next thing you know, one DIs calling for an ambulance and the other two tear downstairs, drop to their knees beside the recruit and keep on yelling at him. "Get up you, pussy, and answer my question: You calling me a liar? Do I look dishonest to you, you weak bitch?"

But I was afraid of Sergeant Allen like nobody else in my platoon was afraid of any DI. Now, try not to lose me here, 'cause this all has to do with the cheating on the range, the lie, rock busting and the point I'm trying to make.

See, one Thursday night, during phase one of training, all us recruits were ordered to sit quietly in the squad bay while, one by one, Allen called us into his office. Each guy went into the office from anywhere between thirty to sixty seconds, and then left and sat back down with the others. We were all polishing our boots and brass. Pretty soon, Private Harrell walked out Allen's office and hollered, "Private Harris, report to the duty hut." I popped up all military-like, as you're supposed to, hauled myself to Allen's office and said, "Sir, Private Harris reporting as ordered, sir."

Allen kept an eight-and-a-half-by-eleven-inch sign on the wall behind his desk. It had two crappily drawn bloodshot eyes on it, and stenciled beneath the eyes were the words KEEP YOUR EYES HERE!! So I locked onto the bloodshot eyes, but I could still see Allen's crew cut, 'cause it was like a black shoe brush sitting on his head. Very noticeable. I could even see the sweat on his forehead, and I could feel those cold black eyes on my throat. "Private Hay-riss," the guy said, "I am required by law to ask you for your religious affiliation so you can be billeted to the appropriate religious service on Sundays. Take your pick, Protestant or Catholic."

Yeah, that's what *I* was thinking, too, 'cause it happened to *be* the case with me. Still is, except I'm not a Muslim or Mormon, like you're saying, but I'm a Buddhist; that is, if you can actually *be* a Buddhist.

No, I'm not joking. I've studied Tibetan Buddhism since high school, but forget about that. I'm talking about this, 'cause this all has to do with why Sergeant Allen ended up hating me. Now, there I was standing in front of this huge hairy DI from North Carolina, and I'm figuring he probably doesn't like blacks as it is. But put a black *Buddhist* in front of him, and you mize well make your black Buddhist a commie vampire coprophiliac child molester, too. I wasn't telling this man shit. But it was a mistake, it turns out. Looking back on it, I should have said, Sir, the private is a Catholic, sir, and been done with it. I mean, at least they burn incense, Catholics, and it doesn't really matter what church you go to, if you study Buddhist thought, anyway.

Okay, instead of saying, "Sir, the private is a Catholic, sir," I said, "Sir, the private can't say, sir."

So the little office got real quiet for a minute and he said, "Why idn't it you cain't say, Private Hay-riss?" And I said, "Sir, it's one of the tenets of the private's religion, that he can't speak his religion's name, sir." I guess, right away, you can see the mistake I was making. That dude musta been thinking, Well, well, weee-ell, what have we got us here, a fuckin black candle-burnin, cowl-wearin cannibal? A nigger Aztec astral traveler?

So he leaned back in his seat, and locked his fingers behind his head. And when the chair finished creaking, he said, "Well, what are some of the other tenets of your faith, Private. I'm sort of a student of religion, though I don't believe in no god."

I said, "Sir, the private doesn't believe in killing, sir."

He dropped his arms to his desktop and leaned forward, and said, "You don't believe in what?"

I said, "Sir, 'killing,' sir."

And then, under his breath, he said, "Pfffuck." Then his voice got loud. "Well, god*damn*, Private Hay-riss, why on earth did you join my Marine Corps?"

I told him I joined to serve my country, but he said, "Serve your—Oh goddamn, boy, if you wanted to serve your country why didn't you join the fuckin army, or the air force? The Corps ain't about serving your country, boy, it's about killing people. It's about body count, son." He sat back in his chair and folded his arms. He started shaking his head. "What are you planning to do in combat, pray your enemy's bullets turn into flowers? Figger they'll bring Frisbees ruther than rifles?"

I didn't have anything to say, of course, and by then I was just thinking, Catholic, sir, the private's a Catholic, okay?

You're damn right I should have; that's what I'm saying, but it was way too late for that, by then. Staff Sergeant Allen just stared at me for a spell, then said, "Are you telling me you wouldn't kill under any circumstances?" And I said, "Sir, it's what the private believes, sir," and he said, he goes, "Private, do you have a mother, I mean is she still alive?"

"Sir, yes, sir," I said, and he said, "Do you have a sister?" I told him I had two. "Well," he said. "All right, private, let's say the Communists invade our country and they break into your home and kill your father, if you got one, and rape your mom and sisters, *before* they kill 'em, Then they burn your house to the ground. All right? Would you feel like killing then, Private Hay-riss, would you feel like cutting their balls off and putting them up their asses?"

Thank you. Who *you* telling? I was standing a short *yard* from the man.

Coburn, son, I was so nervous and shook up, my hands felt cold and my heart was doing triple-time. What was I doing in his Marine Corps? Truth be told, I'd wanted to join the navy, and did go see a recruiter, but on the way out the man's office, this other dude, a little cricket-sized Marine, slick as a photo and about as deep, convinced me the navy was a racist yacht club and I'd never be promoted. "But hey," the man told me, "if you're into swabbing decks and scraping barnacles for four years, fill out the guy's application. No skin off my pecker. I'm just telling the truth." No way was I going to make Allen privy to that. But I did try to tell him about how I could do anything anyone else would do, out of passion, but that wouldn't make it right. I tried to say that probably everybody feels like killing, at one time or another in their lives, but feeling strong about something doesn't necessarily make it right, but I don't know how much of this got out of me, considering my mouth was dry, and considering how hard all that, Sir, the private this and that crap makes it to talk like a human being.

Anyway, before I could finish, he sighed real hard and said, "Stand at ease, boy. Stand at ease." I did but I knew I still shouldn't look him in the eye or even lower my head. Well, the sergeant said, "Frankly, Private Hay-riss—and this is just between you and me. Frankly, I love killing. To me, there's no better feeling in the world than killing somebody. Plain and simple. I served three years in the bush with Third Recon Battalion, before I came to the drill field. Three tours, all volunteer, and by the time I left the bush I had me a hunnerd and nineteen accredited kills." He paused a long time, till the little office filled all the way up with the smell of his Brut, or his Hai Karate, or whatever it was, and then he said, "Accredited." He leaned forward in his chair, then stood, and I could tell his hands were spread flat on his desk. Held his left cheek two inches from mine. Talked right into my ear. His voice got deep and low. I could smell his breath like it was my own. Sweet with tobacco.

"Accredited, Private. I was good at it. Wasn't nobody better at it, in my platoon. I've used Forty-fives, kabars, M-16s, M-14s, M-1s, AK-47s and explosives. I've used branches, bootstraps and steel-toed boots. I've used my bare goddamned hands. I've used my teeth. I don't care what it is, if it'll snuff a son of a bitch, it's for me. Now, you're wasting my time, and I got at least fifty more recruits to interview before reveille. I don't give a flying fuck what you are, or whether you pray on your ass, or on your knees. But when you see that god a yours tonight when you hit the rack, you tell that asshole to send me another war before I start snuffing privates. Now. Take your pick, Protestant or Catholic."

For some reason, I said, "Sir, the first one, sir," and he put me down as Protestant instead of the other. Look, I gotta get back to the shop for a couple hours and bloody up this clean white apron some more. See you next break.

What? Yeah, I'm serious. I don't eat meat these days.

ii

Coburn, what's this I hear about this old lady slapping your hand for packing her stuff too fast?

Really? Too weird. So why didn't you just walk off and let one a the other kids do the order? You don't have to take that kinda crap. What, did my story make you think you were in the Corps?

Hell, that's the kinda thing Sergeant Allen used to do to me after the religion interview. That whole thing made him feel something personal for me, which you really don't want from a DI. You wanna be just another green boot, with a name he can't pronounce, and a face he can't tell from any other. But as soon as he starts feeling something personal for you, the assistant DIs and the other boots start to pick up on it. If they see the DI pick you for the close-combat "dummy" every single time he wants to demonstrate something, the other boots get the idea you're the platoon shitbird, and they can mess with you whenever the DIs look away. And I assure you, they do a lot of looking away in the rifle range phase of boot camp.

Don't really know why, but I think they figure you're

disciplined enough by the end of phase one, and they probably figure it's better to let the boots fight amongst themselves, rather than stay pissed at them. But even at the range, Allen barely let up on me. Like this one morning we're marching to the range, and suddenly Allen says, "Private Hay-riss, you're out of step. Quit messing up my formation," even though it was obvious to everybody I wasn't. Hell, I loved to march, if you can believe that. And I was good at it, too. I loved the chop! chop! chop! sound the boots make, and to really appreciate the sound, you got to be inside the rhythm. You had to be in step. "Sir?" I said. And he said the same thing, so I did the little skip step they teach you so you can get back in step, but naturally I was out of step now, and we marched along a few feet more. "Stop!" he yelled. "Just stop!" which is what a DI says when he's all worked up. You see, when he says that instead of "Platoon, halt!" you're supposed to know you've really screwed up.

So he said, "Stop. Just stop." And, "Hay-riss, boy, get outta my formation." I did get out and I was pissed enough to snatch my rifle off my shoulder and knock his watermelon jaw off his neck. I said, "Sir, the private was not out of step, sir," and he said, "Close your hole, Maggot." And I said, "Sir, the private wasn't out of step till—," but before I could finish, one of the assistant DIs, Sergeant Plumber, zipped up to me and said, "Staff Sergeant Allen just gave you a lawful order, Screw, and you better do it."

I said, "Look, man, I was in step—"

Yeah, I just went off, called the DI "man." I surely did lose my mind.

Then Sergeant Plumber, that little shrew-faced, dog-breath

prick slapped me on the right ear with his left palm and the left ear with his other, and said, "Shut up! Shut up! You want a piece a me, Screw? You want some a this?" and he punched me in the chest, right over the heart, but he was on his heels so I barely felt it. Little prick.

It is. It is illegal, but that never stopped anyone from doing it. Hell, the only thing Plumber did wrong was hit me in front of seventy-seven witnesses, but if you think I or anyone else thought about reporting it, forget it. All it did was open me up to being messed with by everyone. And let me tell you something: after I finished my bends and thrusts, Sergeant Allen told me to get my sorry ass to the end of the formation, and for the first and last time, I let our eyes meet. And the mother let me. He didn't say one word, and I let myself look as long as I wanted to. I could tell he was enjoying himself.

It never got too bad, though, because I choked the devil out this big dope named Polar Bear, this jerk from Alaska, when he came at me one morning in the head.

Yeah, there I was one morning shaving, and this big white boy—head like a bus—lumps over to me and starts this rap about how his brother died over in 'Nam, and how it was pussies like me got good Marines killed. Please. So, this boy racks up his big red knuckles like his name is Mr. G. W. Hope, and like I'm gonna get the thrashing to end all thrashings. I mean, please. I mean, really, like the great pacifist isn't gonna throw hands if some reprobate starts pushing him around. Now that's something that blows the back of my head, Cobes. Like just because you believe in God, a motherfucker thinks you got no will to live. Like you ain't got blood and nerves. Like you don't get annoyed. It ain't but saints who can lotus-pose and burn like a minute steak without a peep. I threw myself his way, clamped my right hand around his tube, and squeezed like I didn't care. Which I didn't.

Sure he hit me; hit me a couple times. Hurt, too, afterward, but I didn't let go till a couple squad leaders yanked me off him. I'm glad they did, too, or he probably would have killed me. The cool thing though, was when they pulled me off him I was struggling for them to let me loose, like they do in the pictures, but man I'm glad those boys had me good. Hell, I acted so crazy, Polar Bear even apologized to me after morning chow, and no one much bothered me after that. Not enough to make any difference, anyway. Besides, when Allen learned I could shoot, he got real nice to me, and what I liked about it so much was that I knew it was like cancer of the dick to this man. That's the only good thing about looking him in the eye that time. I knew how bad it ate him, being chummy with me. I was one of only four qualified expert riflemen in the whole damned company, which is four platoons—three hundred men—and I had the high score, so if he wanted ringers, he pretty much had to come to me first.

Naw, I hate guns, and I wasn't raised around them, but that's probably why I was so good at them. I came to the whole thing like a blank slate. Learned to do everything right, and didn't have to unlearn the wrong stuff. It was kind of fun being good at something I'd never much thought about or cared about, and at the time I liked the way the rifle twitched in my arms, like a woman does when she climaxes.

Well, it's true. And at the time I liked the smell of cordite and hot metal, the way the targets would rise up from behind the mounds, and roll back down a second after you'd squeezed the trigger. And I was always surprised when the score card read anything less than a five, 'cause it happened so rarely. I shot a two-thirty-eight out of a possible two-fifty, and for a while, it's all I wanted to do with my life. So I said sure to the sergeant, and I fired in the prone and the standing positions for one dude, and the kneeling and the standing for this punk named Grice, who was the guy who dropped the dime on us all.

Now that boy Grice was a serious piece a work. Weaselly little shitbird. He had a big nose and bucked teeth, and chewed on the skin around his fingernails till they bled. He constantly got us in trouble for talking when we weren't supposed to, or sleeping through classes. He couldn't keep still. Ever. Even in his sleep. He twitched, jerked, laughed out loud at every lame thought that came into his nut. He was dark-skinned, like a Gypsy, a Greek, an Armenian, so I'm pretty sure a lot of the other recruits and the DIs thought he was a Jew. And lemme tell you, the only military that's comfortable with Jews, it's Israel's. I can't explain that; I just know it's pretty much true. Only thing worse, I guess, would be a Buddhist.

Anyway, about half the time a recruit messed up, they'd punish the whole lot of you, and seven times out of ten, it was pretty much Grice at the bottom of things. He'd washed out of another platoon in phase two 'cause he couldn't qualify as a marksman, and he still couldn't shoot after retraining with our platoon. I hate to admit it, but the pressure let up on me even more when Grice was transferred into our platoon. Well, at least I helped him qualify, but I can't say that was an even trade. But he qualified along with everybody else, and the next week we marched to another camp for phase three of our training, which was all about battle formations, infantry tactics and whatnot.

Well, look, Coburn-bud, I gotta do my last two hours, then close up shop. If you get some free time, throw on a jacket and I can finish telling you about this junk while I'm cleaning up.

Hey, kid, watch out for those old women.

All right, now.

iii

I told you to bring a jacket, man; it's always about thirty-three or -four degrees up in this igloo. Go on, get your . . . Okay, suit yourself. I got some coffee here if you want.

Okay, suit yourself.

All right so yeah, so we were in third phase now, and it's about the best bootsville is gonna get because when the infantry stuff's over, there're only two weeks left, and you spend those back at the Recruit Depot where you began phase one, back at the place where they cut all your hair and brainwashed you, the place with the squad bays that look like a big Florida motel complex. No fond memories, but still it's sort of like coming home after camp. They ease up on you here. You even get to see a movie, if you behave yourselves, and they let you have all the poguey bait you want on movie night: popcorn, Coke, candy bars. The smokers are allowed to smoke more during these last two weeks; the food gets better; you spend more time polishing shoes, buckles, doorknobs, etcetera, than you do bending and thrusting. It's still boot camp, and they still drive the nails in your butt, if they feel like it, but you can see things are winding down, and the DIs' hearts ain't in it. You're getting your uniform ready for final inspection. You clean your rifle till the black metal is gray. They teach you how to tame the hair in your nostrils, your ears, the tip of your nose.

Everything's being fine-tuned now. They want you to feel like that big-dick polished sword in the Marine Corps recruiting ads. You're almost a leatherneck, a devil dog, an all right, high-and-tight, hard-pecker jarhead, who can rhyme like Ali and get a hunnerd and nineteen accredited, that's accredited kills, son.

All right, man, so I sound excited. I am excited. It was an exciting time. I was almost through it. Almost a Marine. Two weeks to go, I had two weeks to go till I could drive a car again, see women, listen to music, read a dozen books if I wanted to. Drink a beer. Hey, I knew I was still enlisted for another three years and nine months, but I knew that military life after boot camp wouldn't be as bad as this had all been. And boot camp is bad, young blood. It's only three months out of your life, but they use the time well. And let's face it, it takes a lot to make a fighter out of kid born in America in the 1950s. As you young bloods say, We was born "phat." And I'm not sure if the Corps ever really succeeded with me. I just don't know. I was never put into the position of having to kill anyone with my own hands.

Hey, toss me that-there scrub brush, buckaroo. Yeah, thanks.

Okay, so Grice qualified with the rifle, but Allen and Plumber and Staff Sergeant Grafton, the only human being among our DIs, just didn't like the dude. No one did. They canned him, basically, for being the cat box of the platoon. He wasn't a likable guy. Even for a so-called nice guy like me he was hard to like. He was still hard to like even when I found out that he was the clown who'd jumped from the third-floor squad bay, and even though he'd washed out twice. I couldn't stand him, even though it was clear he was terrified, that he wanted so bad to be a Marine, probably 'cause he'd always been picked on all his life. I mean, you looked at a guy like Grice and you knew he'd wet the bed till he was eleven years old, and you knew his mom's legs and face were all bruised up, that guys in his high school gym classes put Ben-Gay in his jock strap, that people invited him to parties only to serve him piss-filled beer bottles, and he and his family lived in a home that—

Forget the cleanup on aisle ten. Jack can get it. Let me tell this now, Coburn, before I go home, 'cause I'm not talking about this stuff on Wednesday or any other day. Ask me about it Wednesday, and I'll tell it another way. I'll add new suff, or leave stuff out, and end up God knows where. Hell, I might even disprove my point about lies, and then where would we be? Okay then.

Grice had no place else to go. His home was a cabbage-smelling dump, and he never had a girlfriend. He looked like a Gypsy, and they figured he was Jewish so they treated him like a nigger. He wasn't good at anything. His constant flinching and rippling and nail-biting got under everyone's skin. No, he wasn't good at anything, but he was gonna be a Marine. In the Marines they like to say that you never go any faster than the slowest man, which means that boot camp isn't so hard you can't make it. All you have to do is keep on trying, and you'll make it. I could see that Grice was bound and determined to make it. See, if I could have talked to Allen, and

Plumber and Grafton man-to-men, without all the sirs and privates, and by-your-leaves, I'd have slipped up to them after chow and said, "Hey, fellas, uh, lookee here. Now look, I hope you guys aren't thinking of canning Grice, 'cause, hey, it looks like to me, my brothers, that my boy Grice don't got no place else to go. I mean, think about it. He jumped out a window, but he's still here. Convinced his doctor he wasn't crazy, wasn't stressed, just tripped, just fell, Doc, an accident. No, really.

Never said an unkind word about his DIs either. He's your thinking man's shitbird, see. Laid up in a GI hospital for forty-seven days, foresaw and forgave, and came right back. Washed out in phase two, and he's still here. Nobody likes him; they kick his ass, nightly, daily—or call him names every time you guys look away, but he's *still here.* And, uh, coach Allen, buddy—you ever look at that motherless lizard's eyes? Black, hard, cold as October. Better watch your back, your highness.

I woulda said, Look guys, this punk's been here fifteen—eighteen weeks already, three times longer than a regular phase-two recruit. You cut him loose, and he'll fight back. He'll find some way to still be here, guys, till you make him a bona fide jarhead. But I couldn't say stuff like that. They bum-rushed Grice, most likely without giving it five minutes' thought. And besides, at the time when they were bagging him, I never thought about those things. This is the kind of stuff a guy works out at nights in a place like Corrective Custody Platoon.

It ended up like this.

Roll me that cart, man.

Well, it's just before the last week of boot camp, and it's night. Everybody, except the guys on fire watch, are in the rack. It feels like the holidays, the week before Christmas.

Guys aren't really asleep. They're half asleep, or half awake. Some are whispering to their bunkies about their girlfriends and wives; some are wacking off; some of them are getting high on mouthwash, or by huffing shoe polish. They're looking at the planes taking off from the San Diego airport, which was only about a five-minute walk from the squad bays. You're almost at the end, and even if you couldn't care less about either serving your country *or* killing people, you feel good that you're not guys like Grice who were put back, or guys like this phase-one boy from Platoon 2015, who froze to death in the wheel well of a passenger jet bound for Albuquerque.

So, that night, just before I slipped into full sleep, Private Johnson shook me awake, and said, "Harris. Hey, buddy, Staff Sergeant Johnson wants you up and dressed." And I was up and dressed. Then the sergeant called me and three other men into a small formation outside the squad bay. Allen told us that after Grice had washed it, he ratted to the company commander about the ringers. The C.O., this Captain Hoeg, was fairly new to the company. He hadn't come on till we were halfway through phase three, and I didn't know a thing about him. He had a funny look, though, that bugged me. The thing I most remember about him was his huge calves. Big as rutabagas, these things were. He was built solid and low to the ground, and had pink-pink skin. He had gold hair and gold-rimmed glasses that made him look more like a banker than a jarhead. He didn't look like a regular guy, and I could tell Sergeant Allen thought so, too, 'cause he kept saying things like, "if we stonewall this guy," and "if we deny everything to this guy," and "if we stick together like Marines do . . ." Allen marched us toward company headquarters.

We halted in front of the the captain's duty hut, this Quonset hut I'm sure he'd chose in order to get the feel of the old Corps, and that guts-and-glory, Pokechop Hill nonsense. Allen parked us about fifteen feet from the door, like we were a little Marine hatchback. The first guy walked in scared white, and walked out whiter about five minutes later. The next guy went in and came out the same way. Then came my turn.

The dude's office was cramped and small, and the light was copper. His pink skin and gold glasses were copperish, too, and I noticed he had a cleft in his chin, which made him look even more prep than I'd remembered him. His office was lit with just this one little lamp, one of those things with the green rectangle shade and the brass stem. The whole scene felt like something out of the past, you know, a camp scene from World War I, or one of those Haitian campaigns a hundred years ago, which I'm sure was the effect my boy was shooting for. There was no air in the hut, and even less when the captain slipped one of those skinny brown More smokes from the pack on his desk and fired it up. "Stand at ease, Private," he said after a couple drags, and he tapped some ash into the big brown glass tray behind his nameplate. Then he said, he goes, "Private, I would like to congratulate you on winning company series high shooter." He cleared his throat, and said, "I suppose you know that series high shooter graduates with a meritorious promotion to private first class.

"I've seen your service record, young man, and I can see you're pretty much starting off on the right foot: high marks on all your tests, extremely high IQ scores, excellent proficiency and conduct marks. It all looks good for you, provided we can clear up a little matter concerning an accusation made by Private David. T. Grice that Staff Sergeant Allen led you and several other recruits to fire in the place of certain recruits on the rifle range, last month. Can you tell me anything about that? Does any of this sound the least bit familiar to you?"

And then, Coburn, man, it started feeling like I was in some kind of movie about some guys in a POW camp who were being interrogated by the camp commandant. All this dude needed was a monocle instead of glasses, suede gloves and a foot-long holder for his smoke. Did it sound familiar, he asked me. I was just about to tell him, Suh, hell no, suh—beggin de cappin's pardon—but de private don' know nuttin 'bout dat dar rifle rain stuff, suh—but he said, "Before you answer me, recruit, I want to caution you about the consequences of perjuring yourself in a lawful military investigation of an Article Fifteen offense." He talked about me losing my stripe before I even got it, which meant less money. He talked about the lowering of my pro and con marks, which, believe it or not, I cared about. He told me I had never been under any obligation to honor Sergeant Allen's order, 'cause it hadn't been lawful.

He said, "I can appreciate your being loyal to your DI. I respect it. I encourage it. By now, you're family. We're not investigating you or charging you with anything, but we have to heed the very serious charges leveled against Staff Sergeant Allen, even though they were made by a worthless little shitbird like Private Grice. But you see, even worthless little shitbirds can be right about the wrongs good men do."

Then he started talking about CCP, about what it's like to be there when you've got twelve weeks of basic under your belt. "In some ways it's easier, Private, because you're in great shape, and your mind is more disciplined than it's ever been. I've no doubt you can hack CCP. But there's another side to Corrective Custody for phase-three recruits, that I've seen time and again. You're cockier than the newer recruits, and so you're more likely to mouth off at the wrong time, or lose your temper and do something stupid. It could get worse for you if you screw up there, too. A fall from CCP means a fall into the brig, and after that, Leavenworth Federal Prison, maybe.

"And besides, you could be home in a week," the guy told me. "One week from tomorrow. A ten-day leave, to see home, friends. I know what it's like, Private; boot camp is challenging in the extreme. And those ten days are close as your hands. But if you lie to me, or try to willfully mislead me . . . and I find out about it, I'll have no choice but to sign you into CCP." Then he told me what he'd seen when he observed CCP. He told me everything about the week from hour to hour, so I could feel it in my mind, and practically see it shining off his little gold-rimmed glasses. I didn't know what to do. I didn't know what to do.

Okay, so he carefully rolled his cigarette cherry on the bottom of his ashtray, till it went out in stages, like, with the smoke getting thinner and thinner until it was all gone. And I just focused on the smoke till my brain cooled a little. He cleared his throat again, and folded his hands on his desk. I noticed how long I'd been in his office, and wondered what it was about me made military types blow sermons and speeches. Other guys went in and out, and I was there philosophizing like my name's Bob Confucius. The captain said, "Tell me what you can about Private Grice's accusations, Private Harris."

I didn't know what to do, so I lied, lied my ass off. Lied like a poet. Lied so long and sweet, I'm sure he believed me. It was the sweetest song you ever heard, like Ripple and Smokey Robinson on A.M. radio. *No, sir, the private can't remember the slightest thing. No, your majesty, the private never fired for Privates Grice or Durant. No sire, I don't know nuttin 'bout birfing no bullets. No, my liege, nothing about rifles at all, but can I rub your back for you? You look tired, good King.* What could the guy do? I'd backed up everything the first two guys had said, and evidently the last guy backed me up, 'cause when the captain sent the last guy out, Sergeant Allen looked happy. He marched us back, and told us to get some sleep. "Well done, gentlemen," he told us.

I'm getting to that, just relax.

Well, along about three-thirty A.M. they came back for us, which I wasn't expecting. Allen marched us over and sent us into the office in the same order as before. The captain sat up straighter in his seat than he had before. He never asked me to stand at ease this time, and the overhead light was on, so the room looked pink and bright as the captain's skin. "Private Harris," he said, "let's do this quickly. One of the shooters has confessed to the whole thing, and named himself and you as two of the ringers. This is it, Private Harris, deny it, and you end up in Corrective Custody for at least a week. Choose your words carefully."

Now I want you to listen to me, Coburn, 'cause here's the lie I believed. I know what all I told you about the two kinds of lies, and I still stand behind what I said to you, but when I was there under that dirty pink light, with my body locked at attention, and the captain looking pissed off, and his thick pink fingers shuffling papers around on his desk, and the papers making this snapping noise that's making it hard to think. Hell, man, I just said, "Sir, yes sir, the private knew about everything, sir. The private would like to apologize, sir. The private shot for a couple guys, sir. That's all the private knows, sir." And he dismissed me.

I don't remember being marched back, and I don't remember sleeping that night. Only one guy stood by Allen the whole way, a guy whose name I can't remember. He was the only one of us who went to CCP. I found out later he graduated just one week after we did, and they made him platoon guide, you know, the guy who graduates with the highest pro and con marks, and carries the platoon colors, and gets a meritorious promotion to private first class. None of us guys in platoon 2013 graduated as PFCs. Not even our guide. Staff Sergeant Allen was busted to corporal, and removed from the drill field for about a year. He did come to our graduation, though, in order to shake the hands of the guys he still liked. I acted like I didn't see him, and he did me the same favor. That's the way it should have been. Staff Sergeant Grafton told me that Allen would have his stripes back in a year, and would train new DIs till he could go back to the field. "He'll be okay, Harris. Don't worry about him."

I know you're disappointed, Coburn; I can see it in your face, bud, but it wasn't a lie till now. Not to you. Or even me, really. I'm sorry, man. I was going to tell you the story the way I've always told it. Told it that way to everybody I knew, but this time I just couldn't lift the hammer. It's always been the truth I said, but it was a lie. You see, I can describe CCP so well because I *was* there, in some way. Every year I've added details, made it fuller and realer, and it was mine, Coburn, it was mine. But I'm telling it this way now, kid, because it proves my point better than the old way, those other ways. You're that important to me, man.

No, no, it's not that simple. Understand this. I could taste the cement on my tongue. I could feel sixteen pounds tear up my biceps, my shoulders. I could see my clothes go white with all that dust. The cuff on my ankle cut me, one hot afternoon—I told Muñoz and them in dairy it was a Friday—and it makes me limp to this very day. I've dressed and shaved and fed myself with hands that were calloused by that steel handle. I've showered and walked and chewed to the sound of the two-blast whistle for better'n twenty years. I know how the dust gets between your teeth, how hard it is to brush it away. Can't get it out of my head. It's a lie I've always believed because I lived it.

Goddamn you, Coburn, man, don't look at me like I'm bullshitting; this ain't simple bullshit. Don't go dim on me. This proves my point. I was there. It's taken me years to shake it off, and my back still gets tight when I think about it—about that hammer, about all those nights I couldn't sleep and twisted up my sheets. Even to this day, this second, I still feel ashamed that at the last minute I sided with my brother Grice the shitbird, instead of the Drill Instructor Staff Sergeant Allen, who would have killed for me, I'm sure.

See you Wednesday, kid.

the white boys

i

rain

On Saturday it rained nearly all day. Pea-sized drops battered lawns, streets, the sides of houses. They guillotined leaves from trees and bushes, pummeled these leaves into the grass, plastered them to walls and windows. Ropes of dark green water rushed the leaves down gutters. The green water twisted down drains, or burst into yellow foam onto the grass, forming a miniature system of lakes and streams. Steam hung low to the ground, and overhead, lightning flared through clouds thick as moon dust. Derrick Oates stood at the living room window of his family's new quarters and watched this chaos. He had never before seen rain like this, but then, he was barely twelve and hadn't seen much. He was more accustomed to the stingier rains of the western U.S., where he had done most of his growing up. More like hail, here, he thought, the way it breaks things to pieces, makes birds disappear, eats everything up.

Derrick sometimes liked moving, sometimes he didn't, but there was always something about a new place that excited him in ways he couldn't put into words. Every place smelled different, made his skin ashy or soft, revealed new possibilities in sunsets, fauna, extremes in hot and cold. The sunlight at Mather Air Force Base was hot enough to shatter car windows. The Air Force Academy snowed up to your chest; the acid cold burned ears and fingertips. The tall grasses of Connolly Air Force Base sang with insects, and were perfect for conquistadores, hunters, or Vietnam. If he had been able to, Derrick would have said that every place brought out something new in the world, and in you.

This new rain unnerved him. At times it fell at an angle of perhaps 270 degrees, as though projected by wind, but when he looked at the tops of the trees he could see little evidence of wind. Then suddenly it would fall in lines so startlingly straight that Derrick unconsciously leaned away from the window. Now and then, the lightning flashed with the constancy of a strobe, and the world would go white, but its thunder sounded muffled, as though from behind miles of cloud. Louisiana rain, Derrick thought, falls like lead, like it's shot from a gun.

Some of the boys in Texas had told Derrick that Louisiana would go hard on him. They said they didn't like colored people down there. "Louisiana, Alabama, Mississippi, all them places're southern," John Powers had said. "The *Deep* South, and places like 'at? that's where they had the Civil War." Derrick believed John, not because John had ever lived in the South, but because John was fourteen, and from New York. John spoke with a rattling authority in his hoarse Brooklyn accent, and he always held you with his silver eyes. "Colored people used to be slaves down there," he said. "I figured you knew that."

"I knew that," said Derrick, and he did, but it was in a way that he knew that Christians had once been fed to lions or that Columbus had discovered America. It was a fact of history, a matter for school or church. But John Powers made it sound present, relevant, even urgent. As Derrick listened to him, he couldn't keep from clinching his teeth, and shivering. It was a warm night, full of June bugs, cricket sounds. The warm air smelled of cut grass cooled by the night, and charcoal briquettes gone white. This was well before Derrick's father had received orders for Louisiana, and not long after his return from Vietnam. As far as Derrick knew, they might well be living in Texas for another two or three years. In terms of where Derrick lived now, their talk that night had been merely coincidental. John hadn't been trying to prepare Derrick for a southern journey. It's just that the boys of Randolph Circle often sat and talked for hours on summer nights. They would settle themselves on porches when it became too dark for football, or too late for loud voices. That night, the night John talked about the Deep South, the only boys on John's porch were Derrick and Eddie Lopez, Derrick's best friend. They listened to him closely, as always.

John wasn't the oldest boy on Randolph Circle, but he was the oldest of Derrick's age group, and he was therefore its leader. He nearly always had the final word on everything, was always a step ahead of his juniors. He wouldn't hesitate to pick on any of them, for he always insisted on being right, was quick tempered, and was the biggest of them. But he never really hurt anyone; no one ever left him bloodied or bruised, only humiliated, occasionally to the point of tears. He wore his black hair in a slick DA, and had a smirking gaze that reminded Derrick of Elvis Presley. "Yep, they lynch coloreds down there for nothing. I can't believe you guys didn't know that. They tie 'em up, cut off their balls, burn 'em, maybe they eat 'em, too. I don't know."

"Gyaa!" said Eddie Lopez.

"I don't think so," said Derrick. "My dad's folks live in Tennessee and they don't know anything about that stuff."

"How you know they don't? Maybe they just don't tell you about it. You ever think about that? This ain't the kinda stuff they're gonna tell you, ignoramus." John pronounced the word "ing-no-ray-mus," as Texas boys did, and used the term often. Derrick was sitting with his back against the low brick wall that bordered the porch; his arms were folded over his chest, his legs stretched before him and crossed at the knees. He began to wag his feet after John spoke. He shrugged and said, "Well, I don't think they eat 'em."

"Whadda you know?" said John. "Besides, I don't know if that part is true, but I do know they don't like coloreds down there. All you gotta do is watch the news to know that. Spend all your time watching *The Monkees* and *Get Smart*, and you don't learn diddly."

Eddie chuckled and said, "Get Dumb."

"Get Dumb, you Monkees," said Derrick, and he laughed, too, though he didn't feel like laughing. The barbecue smell on the night air sickened him, and he felt a cold tremor in his chest. He wouldn't let himself think the words, That's what it must smell like. He wouldn't let himself see images of people cooking penises on the grill. He wouldn't imagine charred flesh, or screams, or the nasty laughter of white men. He

118

squeezed his crossed arms tighter together, and held back the shiver, which dissipated everywhere through his body, but would not enter his head, his mind. After a while, he stopped listening to John and Eddie, who were laughing and joking about something else now. He stopped wagging his feet, but kept his arms screwed down tight, till the night wound down and everyone went home.

The rain slackened for a moment, and Derrick looked skyward, but the eaves of the roof blocked his view. Then suddenly the rain dropped by the bucketful and the wind exploded with a momentary gust that bent every tree and bush. Derrick backed away from the window and returned to the bedroom to help his brother unpack and set up.

Derrick found Dean lying on his unmade bed with his hands clasped behind his head, his legs crossed at the ankle. He stared at the ceiling, his brow creased, his tongue making a lump in his cheek. He appeared to be in deep thought, or perhaps just posing as someone in deep thought. Derrick believed he saw mock thoughtfulness on his brother's face; the brows were furrowed enough, but the eyes beneath them had a shirker's glint. "Boy's not working," thought Derrick, " 'cause I was gone so long."

"Took you so long?" said Dean.

"You had a look outside?"

"Yeah, I've seen it and heard it all day. I was up before you."

"How come you're not doing anything?"

"Where were you?"

"I told you I had to go—"

"Well—"

". . . and then I went to look at the rain out front."

"We got windows here."

"You can't see the street from here. I wanted to see the street."

"Mom said we have to be done before supper."

"Dean, you're not exactly killing yourself to get done, I see."

"I'm not gonna do all this stuff while you—"

"Okay, okay, I'm back. . . . Jeez!"

Derrick observed that his brother's head and feet were just inches from the head and foot of the bed. He'd grown at least six inches since last winter, and it was obvious to him that Dean would, in a few years, be taller than him. Dean was taller than any ten-year-old Derrick had ever known, and probably the toughest. But Dean wasn't a bully. He never picked on anyone, never teased or taunted. He kept quiet, mostly, was secretive toward everyone except Alva and Derrick. But perhaps because of his size, smaller boys seemed unable to avoid harassing him. It may have been that they thought he had flunked a grade or two, and if stupid and quiet, couldn't possibly defend himself. But Dean could defend himself. In Texas he blackened more eyes than any boy in the neighborhood. Even many junior high boys feared him. Yet Dean never bragged, never seemed to hold a grudge.

Dean sat up on his elbows, and lifted his knees from the mattress. He said, "All I know is that Mom said we had to be done by supper."

Derrick bent down, lifted a box from the floor to the dresser. "If we're not done in time," he said, "I'm gonna be the one in trouble, not you, so why you worried about it?"

Dean flopped back into the position in which he'd been lying a moment ago, and then thrust himself off the bed and onto his feet. He began removing clothes from boxes on Derrick's bed and placing them in his dresser at the foot of his own bed. They worked in silence for a while, and with great efficiency clothes were folded into drawers, clothes were hung up, dirty clothes were tossed into the corner by the door. They swept, put toys and games in the footlocker, unrolled posters of sports starts, rock stars, Alfred E. Neuman and Spiderman, and taped them to the walls. They plugged in the TV, the record player, the reading lamps and tuned the radio to the local pop music station. They heard "Strawberry Fields," "Incense, Peppermint," "Last Train to Clarksville," "8 Miles High." They shoved books into the shelves of their headboards, slipped the cowboy-motif curtains on their rods and hung them, displayed Derrick's model cars and planes. They made their beds.

Derrick stopped for a moment to gaze out the window. The rain hadn't slackened at all. He sighed and turned to his brother, who was lying on his bed again. Derrick said, "Do you know what the word 'prejudice' means?"

"Sure," said Dean, "I've heard it before."

"It means hating someone because of their color."

"I know, Rick. I said I knew it."

"Yeah, well a bunch of guys at school said they felt sorry for me because Louisiana was a prejudiced state."

"So?"

"And they were smiling when they said it, like, 'Man, are we ever sorry for you, poor sucker.' "

"Derrick, you let those guys get under your skin too much. They're idiots. Didn't you tell me that that guy named Jack Preston didn't know girls don't have dicks?"

Derrick laughed. "Keep your voice down."

"Well didn't he?"

"He *was* stupid but—"

"And you told me about that guy Mike Spivey in your class who was thirteen? And that other guy who was like sixteen?"

"These were different guys. The ones you're talking about barely said two words to me."

"Yeah, but everybody messed with you, practically."

Derrick sat down on his bed and threaded his fingers together and leaned forward. He lowered his head, squinted. He knew his brother's annoyed tone and words had to do with his dislike of housework, and not with the subject matter. He decided to be patient and not lose his temper. He felt that Dean might be the only member of his family, now, who still didn't know where they'd moved. He would talk to Alva about it later. He looked up and said, "John Powers said the same things and he was in junior high. He wasn't exactly my friend, but he was okay." He paused, looked Dean in the eye. "John said they don't like colored people here, and we should be ready for it. And you know Mom didn't wanna move down here, but she told Alva that Dad's only other choice was Japan and he said he'd feel like he was back in Vietnam if we went there. Why you think she wouldn't want to be here, if all that stuff wasn't so? And you ever read *Life*?"

Dean shook his head, smirked a little, shrugged.

Derrick felt his anger rise a bit, and thought, for a moment, of telling Dean to forget it. "Well, didn't you ever hear about that stuff with the dogs and fire hoses when all those people were marching? All that stuff happens down here. All the time. You mean you never heard about that church they blew up?"

"I'm not stupid, Rick."

"You ever heard of lynching? Do you know what that is?"

"Is there gonna be a test?"

"It's like in the movies where they hang a guy for no reason, except maybe he steals something or something, or he's the wrong guy, but they hang him anyway. Without a trial. Well, that's what they still do down here, John says."

"Really?" Dean sat up on his elbows. "Really?"

"Only they do it to colored people."

"Are there pictures of one?"

"Jeez, you act like it's cool."

"Well it is, kind of . . . but not if they really still do it."

"They do; don't worry."

"Not to me. If they try I'll sock their eyes shut."

"Not hardly. They come with guns, dogs, torches. Bunches of people, not just a couple of guys with rope. And sometimes they cut the guy's thing off and—"

"His unit?"

"Watch your mouth. But yeah, they cut it off. And sometimes they burn him, dowse him with gas and light him with their torches."

"Really?"

"Yep."

"Why?"

"Like I said, no reason." Derrick held his hands out, palms up. "Because he's colored." He swallowed hard and looked almost beseechingly at Dean. "John wouldn't make up stuff like that. Nobody would," he said, and sat back a little and threaded his fingers together again. They said nothing for a long time. Derrick stood to turn up the radio when a song by Linda Ronstadt and The Stone Poneys came on. "I hate this song," said Dean. "It's a girl's song."

"It won't kill you," said Derrick. They listened to music till Alva knocked on their door and called them to dinner.

ii

snow

On Sunday, too, rain fell, but it was slacker than yesterday's. Around eleven in the morning the rains grew slacker still, and the air colder, so the rain became sleet, and later still, snow. Both Derrick and his brother Dean squirmed and picked through dinner, and asked to be excused from the table. They wanted to play in the snow before dusk, which was something like an hour away. His father's only answer was to raise his brows and nod to Mrs. Oates, who seemed irritable, stung between the eyes with weariness. "Well," she said, "you either stay in for dessert or go out. You can't do both." "Outside," said Derrick, but Dean looked at him in surprise, then turned to his mother and asked her what the dessert would be. "Banana cream pie," she said, and Dean decided on staying in with his parents and sister for the pie. He tapped Derrick with the back of his hand as Derrick stood to take up his plate and utensils, and said, "Hey, don't forget Disney."

"Oh he'll be in before then," Mrs. Oates said. And he would. There was no question about that. Bath time was at six, Disney at seven, bedtime at eight. School night.

Everything was capped in white and silent. Derrick paced about the whole yard, leaving long green footprints behind him. He hadn't seen snow in the two years they'd lived in Texas and he hadn't expected to see snow here. He'd had the impression that the Deep South was perpetually tropical, fungal, mossy, riddled with bugs. He bent down and scooped a little snow into his hands. He found it much lighter and softer than Colorado snow. It didn't feel as cold. He wished there were much more of it. It dropped in large, puffy, rapidly falling flakes. Derrick stuck out his tongue and tasted a few of them. If it snows here, it'll be okay. Better than Texas, I'm sure.

Life in Texas had been sometimes bitter for him, infrequently good. His father had been on a thirteen-month tour of duty in Vietnam; his mother, overwhelmed with loneliness and the difficulty of raising Dean, Derrick and Alva alone, was given to long periods of sullenness that were sometimes punctuated by angry outbursts. In Sergeant Oates's absence, Alva was thrust into the role of junior parent, which she resented. She took to rolling her eyes and sighing when either of her brothers frustrated her. She dated a boy she didn't seem to like; she took up smoking. Dean had been troubled by a series of lung infections, after being bitten by a rattlesnake. He was far from sickly, though: a month after Sergeant Oates's departure he began getting into fights at school.

Derrick had only one friend—Eddie Lopez, whose father was also in Vietnam. Though he and Eddie had been close, Eddie attended a parochial school in Waco, and there, made other close friends, while Derrick attended Elmott Elementary, a county school, and for reasons he scarcely understood, made no friends. He knew it had to do with his color, to some degree, but he never believed race was the only reason. He blamed himself, his personality.

He had always been extremely shy, timid, contemplative.

Despite his timidity, he smiled easily, and people generally regarded him as friendly, easy to talk to. He was a gifted verbal mimic, like many military children, and despite his black skin, could, to some degree, socially blend with his peers, but he decided that he was too shy for his Texan classmates. This was the thing you faced when you moved to a new place. In one place you felt that the way you dressed was wrong. In another place you felt stupid. In one place everyone you knew commented on your gapped teeth. In another place they couldn't get over how standoffish you were. It couldn't have been only his color. He could only count a handful of times when people had made issue of his color, either for good or for ill, and he had only been called a nigger twice, that he knew of. The first time was in Colorado, at Pine Valley Elementary. He'd struck out for the third consecutive time in a fourth-against-fifth-grade softball game. Though tall for his age, Derrick was reedy and mildly asthmatic, a mediocre athlete. Teammates often accused him of not trying, insisting that he should be able to sink a basket or hit a double because of his height.

There had been no other black children on the playground at the time, and when Michael Rabbit shrieked "Gah! Nigger!" it felt to Derrick that everyone chuckled quietly, approvingly. Michael's white eyebrows seemed to float just off his hot-pink brow, and his head jerked left, "Gah!" then right, "Nigger!" It was only the second or third time in his life he had felt wounded by color, but it felt worse than the other times because so many had heard, many had laughed. He couldn't look at anyone in the face as they left the field. Douglas Phelps, an elfin blond, to whom Derrick rarely spoke, sidled up to him in the line outside the classroom. He tapped Derrick on the shoulder, and said, "Hey, Rick, you know? If someone calls you a nigger like that again? You just look at 'im and say, 'Shut up, you white trash.' You ever hear that word before? White trash? You just say, 'Shut up, white trash.' That'd be neat if you did that."

Derrick looked Doug Phelps in the eye, at his cheery ill-focused gaze, and he knew it would be meaningless to respond in any genuine way. He hadn't, in fact, ever heard the term "white trash," but he knew it wasn't equal to what Michael Rabbit had called him. Instead, Derrick forced a smile, and said, "Yeah, that'd be neat. I'll do it, next time." Doug Phelps slipped his hands into his trouser pockets and grinned. "It's the worst thing you can call a white guy," he said. Mrs. Carroll quieted her students and led them into the classroom.

But his memory of the event was as much sweet as bitter to him because, after recess, his teacher, Mrs. Carroll, read a story about a black boy and a white boy who became friends after a tornado destroys both their homes. When Mrs. Carroll got to the scene where the white boy kneels crying over his dead dog Piper, Derrick's throat knotted. And when she read the part where the black boy brings the white boy a puppy, he thought something would burst inside him. He laid his head on his desk and closed his eyes to stop himself from crying. After the story, Mrs. Carroll gazed around the room that seemed lambent with guilt and goodwill, and said, "Can anyone tell me why these boys would dislike each other?" Jimmy Grimes said, "Because the one boy had a nicer dog . . . well, a smarter dog." "Okay," Mrs. Carroll said, "What else? Anyone?" Cindy Jump said, " 'Cause one boy was good, and one was bad." Mrs. Carroll nodded and replied, "Yes, both did good and bad things." Then Patty Turntine said that it was because the boys were "too different, one was colored, and the other white."

"Good," said Mrs. Carroll, "but why did it take something bad happening to them to make them friends?" Patty Turntine said, "Because when something bad happens to people they feel the same way." Mrs. Carroll let the room lie silent for a spell, and then said in a voice a little tight with emotion, "Yes . . . That's good. Yes."

Derrick felt this as an almost holy moment. His face felt warm, and his body trembled. There was a feeling both heavy and light in his gut, and he felt like standing and walking up to Mrs. Carroll. He wanted to press his face to her body, and be held in her arms. He felt light as steam, heavy as earth. Patty Turntine was an angel, Mrs. Carroll a saint, everyone in the room glowed with a pink that Derrick thought he could see. Beneath his consciousness, he understood that, bad as he had felt after the game, these feelings, this holiness wouldn't have spread itself throughout the room that day if Michael Rabbit hadn't called him nigger; his color spun tornadoes wherever he went. It tore down houses—and houses, however good they were, however secure, created separateness.

There had been no such moments in Texas. For the most part, his teacher and fellow students ignored him. They behaved as though they neither liked nor disliked him, though there was one boy, a huge, hairy, acne-riddled sixteen-year-old sixth-grader named Oakley, who harangued him daily, and wouldn't be satisfied, it seemed, until Derrick accepted his challenges to fight. But Derrick never did fight Oakley, for Oakley had been expelled for fighting another boy.

They'd lived in Texas for about a year and a half, and two months after Sergeant Oates's return from Vietnam, he received orders to Barksdale Air Force Base, Louisiana. Everyone was ready to leave. The family felt as though it had lived with a cyclone, and they left Texas without a backward glance. All that Derrick missed was playing with Dean, Eddie and some of Eddie's friends in the fields behind Derrick's house. Their quarters had lain on the border of the base and a farmer's property. The boys of his neighborhood were drawn to the farmer's land like the birds to the grasses that grew there, like the frogs to the creeks and ponds, like the snakes, the turtles and the insects to the marshes. They played war, mostly; they hunted the fauna, skipped rocks on the water, and he and Eddie Lopez sat for hours on the banks of the pond and talked about the war, about the protests against the war, about letters from their fathers, about hippies, and drugs, about civil rights and the Apollo missions, sports, sex, parents, siblings. Derrick would miss those things, but he wouldn't miss school.

Soon, the snow stopped falling and the neighborhood became even quieter than it had been. Derrick suddenly grew bored with the confines of his front yard and scanned the street northward and southward. But as he started for the street, his mother's voice halted him. "Rick," she said, "don't go anywhere, son. Your father might have something for you to do later on."

Derrick turned and saw his mother on the stoop, her arms folded against the cold. "Yes ma'am."

"Stay where we can see you."

"Yes ma'am."

He went no farther than the curb, but considered going farther, despite his mother's wishes. Prob'ly thinks I'll get lost. Always thinks I'll get lost just because of that one time.

Jeez. I was seven. And he hadn't really been lost, though he'd gotten home from school nearly an hour late. The fact of the matter is that he'd pissed his pants. He'd simply misjudged his need to relieve himself before leaving school. He spent the better part of an hour melting snow in his hands and letting it fall on the crotch of his pants. He planned to sneak into the house, and stuff the jeans into the bottom of the hamper, change clothes and greet his mother with the news that he'd been forced to walk through drifts, and that the snow had melted on his pants. "I put 'em in the hamper already," he'd tell her.

His mother met him at the door that afternoon, and he could tell she'd been crying. But Portia Oates wasn't the kind of woman to throw her arms around some late-arriving boy. Derrick knew his mother wouldn't be found pacing the living room, or on the phone with the military police. Most usually she would bellow, toss things around—dish rags, cooking utensils, laundry—slam doors and drawers shut, snap them open, forestalling her urge to cry with the furious movements of her body. She was a tall woman, solidly built, with a loud sharp laugh and a violent streak hot as a match. Derrick had often heard her described as handsome, and he himself thought her smile more beautiful than anything he had ever seen in any person. Yet, mostly, she was an angry blur to him. She moved in quick smooth arcs, as though her every move had been choreographed and rehearsed.

Derrick feared her, naturally, and crept past and around her with his head cocked slightly to the left and his shoulders drawn up. He knew that she loved him, and because of this, he tried to bend himself to her will, appealing to her with eyes shaped by what he thought was innocence. He kept the eyes large and looked straight into her eyes when she spoke, and shifted his gaze down when he replied to her. Now and then, she treated him with tenderness, but she tended to treat him so after she whipped him, and he, in turn, treated her as one would treat the weather: with awe, or indifference, or a morose helplessness.

As soon as Derrick had stepped up to the door, his mother jerked it open, said, "Get in here, boy," and stormed off to the kitchen. He followed her there. She settled herself against the counter, her arms and ankles crossed. Snow clung to the window behind her, and she turned to look at it as though she could see through the snow and into the yard. "I see you finally got yourself home," she said, and she turned her face to him.

"I got lost."

"I see. Did you track snow in my house?"

"No ma'am." Derrick stared at his mother's folded arms and added, "I don't think so." He felt hot under the car coat, the sweater, the heavy plaid shirt, the T-shirt, and his crotch itched to the point of burning, steeped as it was in piss and melted snow, yet he made not one move to make himself more comfortable. He was afraid to do anything that would make it appear that he wasn't fully attending his mother, and he didn't wish to draw to himself any special attention.

"Where's your lunch box?"

The question took him by surprise, and he couldn't hide the panic in his eyes. His voice trembled. "I took a bag today."

His mother herself looked taken aback for a moment, but her eyes quickly registered the memory of packing his lunch bag into his book bag that morning. Derrick relaxed just a touch, but then she suddenly set one arm akimbo, and his stomach tightened. "Where were you?"

"I tried to take a shortcut, and I got lost because of the snow."

"A shortcut where?"

He pointed vaguely toward the door. "That way."

"*Where!*"

"On the wrong street—"

"You don't think I know that!" Her voice shook. Derrick could see that she was on the verge of tears. She turned from him in what he thought was disgust. She opened up the hot water, and steam rose up around her face and billowed off the frozen window. "Damn kids. Wear me out. And all this damn snow. Coulda been dead out there. Look like he don't even care. Don't a one of 'em care. Not one." She jerked around. "Go to your damn room, boy! Standing around like a damn . . . Go!"

Derrick hovered by the curb for a minute and gazed at a light blue Rambler wagon parked only a half dozen paces away. He approached it and rather mindlessly began scraping snow off the hood. He squeezed the snow between his palms, compressing it into a thin wafer, his life lines imprinted on it. He then collected more snow from the hood, intending to make a snowball, but there was barely enough to make one the size of a golf ball. He wondered whether enough snow had fallen on his entire yard for a decent snowball. He scraped a bit more of the fake-feeling snow from the Rambler's hood and squeezed it until it began to drip from his fist. Water fell on the hood and rolled to the ground. He thought again about the time he'd pissed his pants.

The storm had grown stronger in the evening. He ate dinner, and skipped his homework, assuming there'd be no school the next day. He watched *McHale's Navy*, bathed and went to bed. Pretty soon he forgot all about pissing himself, his mother's annoyance. Dean had already been asleep for an hour, and so Derrick lay in bed and listened to the sounds of the television, his parents' and sister's conversation, the sound of the wind whipping snow against the house. He felt good. Soon, sleep rippled across his brow, and his bed began to float.

But abruptly the light snapped on, and he felt himself yanked by his ankle from bed. His head hit the floor, and he squinted up at his mother, who, without releasing his leg, lashed him with a belt. It was some dozen strokes before Derrick felt the bite of the leather, or heard his mother's words sharp in his ears. "Keep y' hands down, keep y'... Move y' hands!" He wouldn't keep his hands down, and more than that, tried to use his left foot to break the grip she had on his right ankle. She jerked him nearly vertical and swung him to the right, and his head hit the leg of his bed. He yelped, cupped his palm over the lump that rose there, but steadily occupied his other hand with defending himself from the belt. It was all but pointless, of course, so he clutched the bed frame and tried to pull himself underneath the bed, but his mother muscled him into the open each time he tried, and she lashed with greater fury. He couldn't gather what he had done to deserve this beating, but before he could so much as protest, or explain or lie, his mother had spent herself. She released his ankle, and turned to the door. She bent over a pile of laundry in the hallway, snatched up the jeans and threw them at Derrick. "Next time you piss your pants like an infant," she said, "take the damn things off and put 'em on the floor *next* to my hamper. Whole pile of clothes smells like your pee now."

She flicked off the light, and shut the door. Derrick climbed back into bed, covered himself and tried to stifle his sobs.

As his body relaxed, his wounds heated and swelled, became distinct from one another, rather than the sheet of undifferentiated pain they had been seconds after the beating. Each welt uncurled like a vine, became almost alive with intensity. He felt seven along his back, a couple on his arms and chest, one on his chin, one that ran from his throat to his ear. His head throbbed beneath the knot the leg of the bed had left there.

The whole time the lights had been on Dean hadn't moved, but Derrick knew his brother was awake. He knew Dean lay silent and still out of fear, and Derrick felt the usual humiliation, which for him felt most acute when the beating was over, and a kind of ultra-silence filled the whole house; bad feeling lay along the floors like cold air. There were times when the only sound in the house was the sound of Derrick's hiccuping.

If he sobbed too loudly and too long in the aftermath of a beating, his mother would threaten to really give him something to cry about; she'd return to his room brandishing the belt; she would shake it in his face and he would stifle every sound until his body would convulse. But when she'd shut the door again, Derrick would charge into the closet, gather all the coats around his head and scream until his throat shut tight. That night, however, he mastered himself, locked himself down in less than a minute, and it left the room so quiet that he heard what sounded like Dean's sniggering. He sat up, turned on his reading lamp and said, "What's so funny?" Dean said nothing. He lay on his side, facing the wall, neither moving nor speaking, so Derrick repeated the question.

"Nothing," said Dean, and by the timbre of his voice,

Derrick understood his brother was crying. "What's wrong? Are you okay?" he said.

"I'm scared," said Dean. "She scared me."

"She's not gonna spank you, Deano."

"I know," said Dean, but his sobbing grew more intense.

Derrick slipped from bed and sat next his brother. He didn't know what to do beyond that, at first, but eventually he lay down next to Dean and wrapped an arm around him. He felt strange, at first. He'd never hugged his brother, hadn't held him since Dean was four days old, fresh from the hospital. "Stop crying," said Derrick. But Dean began to cry with yet greater intensity, and for a very brief moment, Derrick felt angry. For that moment, he felt the impulse to shake his brother, or clamp his arm round his throat and hiss, *Idiot! Shut up. She whipped me, not you!* But instead, he breathed deeply and drew closer to Dean. Tears filled his own eyes, but he blinked them back. "I'm the one they don't like, Deano."

"I know."

"They've never spanked you, just me."

"I was asleep."

"I know."

"I didn't know what happened. I thought she was gonna spank me, too."

"You didn't do anything."

"I thought I did."

"What's that supposed to mean?"

Dean gasped and exhaled. His body grew lax. "I don't know," he said. "I thought I did."

"*Did* you do something bad? I won't tell."

"I don't know. I don't think so."

135

"Well, I did. I peed my pants; then I put my pants in the hamper."

"On purpose?"

"Pee, or the hamper?"

"Did you *pee* on pupose."

Derrick chuckled. "Why would I pee on purpose?"

"Then how did it happen?"

Derrick rolled onto his back, and laid his hands on his chest. "I guess I was too cold. I just couldn't hold it." He sat up, tapped his brother's arm with the back of his hand. "Hey, Dean," he whispered, "you think I should wear a diaper?"

"No!"

"I'm just kidding."

"You're not a baby!"

"Not so loud, Dean. I was just joking. I was talking about me, not you. Why you so mad?"

"Why don't you hit her back?"

"Are you nuts? She's ten times bigger, and Daddy's twenty times bigger. I can't hit back; they'd kill me."

"Well, you're not a baby."

Derrick didn't know whether Dean was angry with him or their mother, or whether he was angry at all, but he was relieved he'd stopped crying. He returned to his own bed, covered himself and said, "I could drink soda from a baby bottle, too. That'd be kind of neat."

Dean giggled. "Shut up."

"And I could wear a big ol' bonnet."

"No, a big bow in your hair!"

"Shhh! Mama's still up." Derrick turned out the lamp. "And those white baby shoes, you know, the ones that look like boots? And Daddy could push me around in a giant stroller."

They laughed in whispers, whispered the joke for fifteen minutes, turned it to every absurd angle that struck them. When they exhausted the joke, they turned to other matters, reveled in silliness until they heard the television shut off, and Alva wish their mother a good night. Dean was asleep in two or three minutes, but Derrick lay awake until the house grew so silent that the wind sounded like sirens and thunder.

iii

neighbors

The Louisiana snow dripped from Derrick's fist and he said in a whisper, "Not too smart, boy. Not too smart." And then someone behind him said, "Excuse me," so Derrick turned around, his eyes big. "Sir?" Derrick said. He faced a tall, broad man with doughy skin, a crew cut and a thick, short mustache. Veins stood out blue and stark in the middle of his large, square forehead and his temples. His two-day beard prickled blue out of fat cheeks, and he may have been smiling, or he may have been sneering, or he may have been wincing against the cold. Derrick couldn't tell. The man said, "I'd appreciate it if you wouldn't mess with my car."

"I was just trying to make a snowball."

"All this snow, and you pick my car? What about the ground? What about your own car?"

"I don't know."

The man folded his arms over his chest. "Where you live, Sport?" The man had an eastern accent, what Derrick thought of as a New York accent. "You come down from Pelican?"

"No sir. Four-oh-nine First Street East."

The man arched his brows. "Next door? Don't see no van, Sport, you sure?"

"We got here day before yesterday."

"What's your name, Sport?"

"Derrick."

"Uh-huh. Where you from?"

"We just came from Connolly Air Force Base in Texas."

"Connolly. I see. They think it's okay to mess with people's cars in Texas?"

Derrick looked at the man's fat mustache, his tiny ears, his fat pink jowls, his tiny wet mouth. He decided he not only disliked the man, but hated him. He looked past the man and saw his father standing behind the screen door of the house. His father then stepped onto the front porch. He felt both relief and anxiety cut a line from his navel to his heart. "Derrick," his father said. He had spoken in his usual deadpan tone. "Sir?" Derrick said. "That's my dad." As he stepped past the man, the man spun round and called out to Sergeant Oates, "Hey, Sarge, I'd just appreciate it if Sport here'd kinda watch it with the old wagon. You know how kids are."

Sergeant Oates smiled and waved at the man. He nodded. "That's right, bud." And when Derrick walked past him and into the house, he followed the boy, and without another word or a backward glance, shut the door. Sergeant Oates pointed to the kitchen and said, "Siddown, pardner." There in the kitchen, Derrick's mother and sister washed the dishes, papered cabinets, emptied boxes. The two of them had tight-mouthed looks that to Derrick seemed unreasonable. He'd done nothing. This was going to be about nothing.

His father had been polishing his shoes, and so the smell of polish and lighter fluid mixed with that of cooked food, dish soap, floor wax and the smoke that curled from the end of Mrs. Oates's Pall Mall. The room felt stuffy, hot. Derrick could scarcely breathe. He imagined telling his father that the heat and odors were making him ill, and that he was going to bed. Nothing happened, Daddy. I'll tell you about it tomorrow. After school. I'm tired. G'night.

Of course, no such thing would ever happen in the Oates home. His parents were quick to note the slightest gesture of anger, impudence or frustration, and quick to suppress it. So much as a half-clenched fist, a scowl, a word spoken too forcefully, could escalate their anger fivefold. Neither Anton nor Portia Oates knew, from their children, backtalk, whining, cursing. When summoned, they appeared; when dismissed, they left. They were as disciplined as troops, and if the Oateses were ever pleased with their children, they seldom expressed it.

Sergeant Oates sat down, slipped his hand inside a shoe and took up his polish rag. The yellowish light of the room glowed off his bald head, the toes of his shoes, the gold of his watchband. He was taller than his wife by a head and a half, and lighter skinned by two shades. When he was angry, his forehead and cheeks went amber, and his green eyes sharpened enough to make Derrick feel pierced through the brain. His father seemed to read his mind, but wasn't always right, while his mother assumed that most of what he said was a lie, and she wasn't always wrong.

"Stood at that window for five minutes," his father said, "and I watched you messing with that man's car."

Unlike his mother, his father always took his time working from calm to angry. His anger, therefore, wasn't as unpredictable, but he could wield a belt just as handily and hit twice as hard. He was a drinker, but was only violent when sober. When drunk, he was sentimental and quiet. When drunk, he dared optimism, forgave enemies, even white people, and allowed himself to dream. When sober, he lived fully in the present, sharp-eyed, wary, grim. He thought only of what he had to do, and if that be to beat his son for disobedience, stealing, lying, for neglecting his chores, he would—though he preferred not to. Beating children made him feel bad, and he took his time about such things perhaps to get a better feel for the degree of punishment he must administer. He'd circumlocute, philosophize, stalk his prey like a cat.

"What'd I tell you about fooling with other people's property? What'd I tell you I'd do if you brought trouble to this house?"

"I was wiping snow off the car—"

"Wiping—"

". . . so I could make a snowball." Derrick's voice was quavering, and he hated this. He kept telling himself that this was about nothing, and tried to breathe more deeply.

Mrs. Oates said, "All that snow on the ground, Derrick, all that snow on the ground and you—"

"I can handle it, Portia."

"Well handle it, then," Portia said, and slammed a cabinet door shut. She continued to speak, half aloud, about hoodlums, troublemakers, liars, thieves. Sergeant Oates carefully set the finished shoe on the floor next to the one he was yet to do. He sat forward in his chair and laid one large hand on the table, drummed his fingers once, twice. "What'd I tell you I'd do, if you brought trouble to this house, boy?"

Skin me alive, thought Derrick, knock me into next week, beat me black-and-blue, coldcock my fuckin head, tear my ass up, but he said, "A spanking?" He wanted to scream at his father, storm from the room. It was all so stupid to him. He'd done nothing. Usually, he preferred that his father take his time this way, for the longer he took, the less likely the chance of a beating, but tonight his father's slowness crushed the air from his lungs, made him tremble.

Black polish lay under Anton Oates's broad fingernails, and there was a streak of it on his cheek. His head glimmered under the yellowish light and Derrick understood that the house really was too warm. It wasn't only fear that made him perspire so. "I'd get a spanking if I did that," he said.

"You got that right, bud."

"Whole yard full of snow," said his mother, "and you gotta mess with that man's car. Son, you don't even know him. Don't even know him."

"Portia, let me talk to the boy."

"Daddy, I didn't do anything."

"Boy's bored, is what it is," said Portia. "Well, young man, there's plenty left to do around this house to keep boredom at bay for a week."

The sergeant said, " 'I didn't do anything' is not why the man went out there to talk to you. You copy?"

"Yes sir."

"Uh-huh, well, the point is whenever you do something that arouse suspicion, you did do something. You made somebody notice you for the wrong reason, buddy, you see what I'm saying?" The sergeant smiled suddenly, and abruptly withdrew the smile. This was his habit when he spoke with instructive authority, but every time it happened (and it appeared to just happen; it seemed reflexive rather than conscious) Derrick felt himself return his father's smile, and when it would vanish quickly, he'd still be smiling. It embarrassed him. He felt as though his father intentionally fooled him, mocked him. He despised this in his father. But, of course, he never let himself show it.

"Yes sir, I see," Derrick said.

Portia said, "Go check on your brother." She thumbed toward Anton Oates. "That is," she said, "if your father's finished with you."

Sergeant Oates crossed his legs and leaned back. "Don't you embarrass this household, young man. You know what they'll say about us."

Derrick knew what they'd say. He knew what his father meant. The doughy man next door would say, That colored boy was tryin to steal my car, the little bastid. Them people steal, you know. The man would say that them people are lazy, and acted stupid even if they weren't. He would say they went to school with cotton in their hair, and their shoes unshined, with ashy skin and untucked shirts. He would say they couldn't make their beds, and they let dust balls collect under the furniture in their bedrooms. They forgot to dump the trash, and didn't sweep the sidewalk adequately after their fathers cut the grass. They had trouble getting up on time for school or chores, and they lost nice things, or broke them five minutes after getting them. They didn't care about a nice home or good grades or saving money. They lied like devils. They had to be watched every moment, couldn't be trusted any further than they could be tossed. They brought embarrassment to their homes, and would end up on skid row if they didn't shape up. Maybe military school would be good for them because spanking didn't seem to work. There was no question that Derrick knew what they'd say, and he told himself nearly every day he'd give them no reason to. "Yes sir," he said to his father.

" 'Yes sir,' what?"

"I know what they'll say. They'll say we're no good."

His father looked straight into his eyes, and drummed his fingers on the tabletop one, twice, and nodded. "Go on, then," he said.

iv

river city

As Sergeant Eugene Hooker stepped into his living room, he flicked a little melted snow from his mustache and said to his wife, "And so it begins." Tonya Hooker knew he was tired, knew she should send the boys to their rooms, shut off the television, pat the empty cushion next to her and let him spend himself for the—what was it?—six or seventh time on this subject. She knew she should listen to him, but since Friday he'd been grousing about the colored family as though the Devil himself had moved next door. She was sick of it. What more was there to say? He'd said that they should be living on Pelican Street with the rest of them, and she reminded him that this was the only base at which they had ever been stationed where segregation still lingered. He would begin to talk about his teen years when his parents split and his mother moved back to Baltimore with him and his sisters. He'd tell her that his life had been perfect in Springfield, where "You saw them all the time, but almost never had to deal with them."

But in Baltimore they lived on almost nothing, in the midst

of them, those people, who stole from them, beat him up on his way to and from school, who harassed, terrified and humiliated his sisters nearly every day, and who had the nerve to send one of their number forth to marry his mother. His mother was as good as dead to him from the moment she brought that man home, and their sons knew nothing of her. "Your grandmother was a drunk," he'd tell the boys, "and she drank herself to death."

Tonya herself had met Mrs. Hooker only once, in May 1951, at Baltimore-Washington International Airport, a week after their wedding. The meeting lasted for thirty minutes, but wouldn't have taken place at all if not for Tonya's insistence that she be allowed to meet Mrs. Hooker. "If she's your blood, she's mine," she said, "and I just wouldn't feel right about this marriage if I never got a chance to see what kind of family I've married into." Sergeant Hooker was, as he put it, "goony with love," and if he'd been in his right mind, he would have refused her demand. He conceded, but told her that this would be the last time either of them would ever see her again, and the last time he'd speak of her or allow her name to be spoken in his presence. Before their engagement, Eugene was given to lengthy monologues on his history. It was painful talk, full of every cruel thing children suffer. With each story she loved and pitied him more and more. It was a history she had neither heard of nor imagined: a father who went crazy and lived on canned food in their basement, a sister who lived in Germany and never wrote or called, another sister who married an ex-pimp who took her to Las Vegas. And his mother, who once watched their kitchen burn for five minutes before calling the fire department, who came at him with a poker for mouthing off to her, who divorced the poor son of a bitch in the basement, moved them to a colored neighborhood in Baltimore and married a colored butcher.

The meeting was awkward and sad, as Tonya remembered it, but Mrs. Hooker was surprisingly youthful, humble and loving toward her son. Tonya had imagined she would be big as her son, red-eyed, and dressed in purple satin. She thought she would smell of whiskey and stale smoke, and talk like a Negro, but she was a petite, pale woman with silver-flecked black hair and olive-black eyes. She had the faintest hint of a mustache that somehow made her more lovely. She wore a simple pale blue dress, and a matching scarf, a car coat, white socks and cordovan penny loafers. She threw her arms around Eugene and wept so convulsively that Tonya wept, too, and she thought her heart would break when she saw Eugene's face. He clinched his jaw, flared his nostrils, struggled to gain enough control over himself to smile, or appear cool, or reveal the hatred, shame or pity he seemed to be trying to achieve. On the flight there, he'd said he would "chat with her, see what the old broad's been up to for the last four and a half years, you know?" He thought that if he had to go he could at least crush her with indifference. But for nearly the whole of the thirty-minute meeting, he scarcely said a word, as though one too many syllables would impel him to wail like a mourner.

When mother and son were composed enough to speak, they exchanged pleasantries as though they were high school acquaintances who'd run into each other in the middle of an errand-filled day. This made the whole event all the more painful for Tonya, who felt a little responsible for their reticence. They exchanged more words while backstepping than they did while they'd embraced. "You've put on weight," Mrs. Hooker said. "You look like a grown man."

Eugene replied, "Yeah. Yeah, I guess. Oh, hey, did you ever put the new roof on the house? I been thinking about that."

"Geno, that was years ago. Years ago."

The last words he ever said of her, he said while buckling himself into his seat, five minutes before takeoff. "What a fucking wasted life." Soon, they were in the air again and off for Springfield to see his father, his aunts and grandmother, and a week later, they were back in South Dakota at Ellsworth Air Force Base, where they would live for the next five years.

They lived only a few miles from her family in Villa Ranchaero, so her first few years of military life were not much different from the lives of her former classmates. Though Tonya knew better, she sometimes let herself believe this would be their life forever. But it seemed so perfect, just as she'd always imagined it would be. Eugene Junior was born in '52, and Devon in '54 and Garret in '56. Eugene spent most of his free time at home working on his cars, and helping her with the boys. She had a job at the A&W, and belonged to a women's archery club. They spent most weekends at her parents' home, and never missed church. Nothing worried them or oppressed them in any way.

After Tonya married him, Eugene rarely spoke of the things that bothered him. When he did, she learned to keep her opinions to herself, ask him no questions, merely listen to him till he talked himself out. He seemed to have few political opinions. He was silent about his family, and quiet about difficulties at work. He never talked about his hatred of black people because there were virtually no blacks in western South Dakota at the time—except for the handful stationed at Ellsworth—and Eugene rarely saw them, had neither the reason nor the desire to speak to one. By the time they left South Dakota, Tonya had entirely forgotten the issue.

From 1956 to 1962, they were stationed in Japan, and from '62 to '65, they lived in London. After London came Louisiana, and as the years went by, Eugene grew more silent, and their marriage, which she thought of as still very solid, became less lustrous. They saw her family only once a year, and he would shrug at her homesickness. His father died while they were in Japan, and he grew dour. There were no women's archery clubs in the places they lived after South Dakota, and Eugene discouraged her from working outside the home. But the core of their family life remained undamaged by the many vicissitudes of military life. She still thought of her life as full, rich and good.

So she was a little surprised at Eugene's vehement reaction to the new family next door. It had been only three days, but she was so full of his speechifying and pacing and window-gazing, that she began to feel as though things had always been this way, and she wearied of it. She watched him pace the living room and hated his every movement, hated every grunt and sigh, every whispered curse word. She stood up and turned off the television. "Boys," she said, "Daddy and Mommy—"

"No," said Sergeant Hooker, "I want the kids to know. They're right up on our doorstep now, and I think the boys ought to know what they're up against."

"Gene, I really think—"

"Everybody on the couch. Come on, Garret, up here, Sport. Come on. Junior, why don't you switch on that lamp there, son, so I can see you guys. Little dark in here."

"What'd we do, Dad?" said Garret.

"Nothing, Sonny. Daddy just wants to talk to us."

Tonya waved Garret to her, and patted the cushion to her left. When he sat, she folded her arm around him and hugged him close. She meant to comfort herself, rather than him. Eugene smacked his hands together and rubbed them as if to warm them. He lifted his heels from the carpet, and bounced them a bit. "I want you boys to listen close," he said, " 'cause we got trouble right here in River City." He smiled at his joke and shook his head in embarrassment when no one returned his smile. "Okay, boys, just a minute ago I chased off this colored kid from messing with the car. He was making like he was scraping snow off the hood so he could make a snowball.

"If you boys knew niggers like I know niggers, you'd know the boy had no more interest in snowballs then I have in growing horns." The older two boys laughed, and Sergeant Hooker felt encouraged, so he went on in a somewhat more relaxed manner. "I know for a fact," he said, "it's in their nature to steal, just like it's a dog's nature to chase cats—"

"Gene," said Tonya.

"Tonya, don't interrupt."

"Gene, we agreed we wouldn't use curse words around the boys."

"I haven't used one—"

"We want our boys to use 'colored' or 'Negro.' Remember, Gene."

"Noted. Can I go on?"

"I didn't mean to interrupt."

Sergeant Hooker answered by clearing his throat, and said, "Colored people steal, they lie, they skate at their jobs, they're not very clean and they gamble. It's not that white folks don't do the same things, it's just that they do it less, or less so than coloreds. I don't know all the reasons why, but I grew up around them from the time I was about Garret's age till I joined the service. This was in Baltimore, years back. I went to a school that was something like sixty percent colored, and in a neighborhood that was almost a hundred percent colored. I had to fight every day, practically, to defend myself, and your aunt Carolyn and aunt Tina. They were the worst years of my life.

"Now, uh, now you boys know we've spent a lotta your growing-up years in foreign countries. Well, your dad did that on purpose, understand, because I've wanted you to grow up in places where there's the fewest niggers possible. Sorry, Tonya. I meant to say Negro.

"But, the thing is, boys, the thing is, a lot has changed in this country in the years we were gone. Colored people, lately, as you can see on the TV and the papers, have been getting louder and more dangerous every day. They're growing the bushy hair, and turning communist. They're killing white people by the hundreds, turning our kids on to drugs, and pimping our girls—"

"Gene."

Sergeant Hooker reddened, and bowed his head for a moment. He knew Tonya wouldn't be interrupting him this way if she weren't surrounded by their sons. He shrugged, lifted his head. "The boys have to know this stuff, Tonya. It's for their own good, for their future. How long we gonna protect 'em. How long we gonna . . . They do terrible things, those people, and it's in their nature to do these things. I mean, maybe you think I'm being hateful, here, but I'm not. I don't hate anyone, not coloreds, or communists, not cowards. If anything, I feel sorry for 'em. Colored people do what they do because they can't help it, like the way the Indians up in South Dakota used to drink, or the Japanese bow. That boy next door was casing my car, Tonya. Three days here and already he's looking for trouble." He paused, looked away from Tonya, then, for no particular reason, looked at Devon. "I know, even though she's never said so, your mom doesn't really agree with me on this 'cause when we were in London she was friendly with Sergeant Brophie's wife."

"She was my best friend."

"She was her *best* friend, okay? But the colored woman isn't as bad. She works hard, and has to raise her kids, those that have 'em, anyway. Some of 'em work in ways and places that you're too young to understand, right now, but there are some good ones. And it's true that as far as the males are concerned, there's some good ones, too. Brophie wasn't a bad guy. He was pretty squared away. But you don't get to know a certain race of people by meeting one or two of them and making up your mind about 'em. Exceptions don't make the rules. What it takes is getting to know hundreds of 'em—which I have—and which I hope none of you have to do. Take your dad's advice: pick up your stuff from the yard, when you're done with it. Don't let me see you leaving your bikes unlocked, or leaving my tools laying around, 'cause I guarantee you, things will be disappearing from around here.

"And don't let 'em intimidate you. They like to do that. They're good fighters, but they can be beat just like any other man. But if they don't start anything with you, don't you dare start anything with them. Just the same way I've taught you about dealing with white people. It's not worth getting expelled from school or locked up. They're not our enemies any more than water and oil are enemies. Just keep yourselves to yourselves and let them go on their merry way. If they say good morning, you say good morning. If they wanna play in a neighborhood ball game with you, and the rest of the fellas, well, let 'em play, but they don't come in for no water, or to use the bathroom, or anything else. They don't come in the house, period. Are we clear on that, gentlemen?" He nodded after the boys told him they understood, and he set his arms akimbo. "When your dad does his job for the country, he does it for them, too, like the sergeant next door does it for you. You are not to act disrespectful to the sergeant, or to his wife. You're to remember that Dad's promotions don't just depend on how he does his job, but on how his family does theirs.

"You're not to do anything that would bring embarrassment to me or my career. I will not lose the stripes I've earned because you boys have been caught acting like them. Like the people next door."

He paused, looked each boy in the eye and slowly nodded. He couldn't think of anything else to say. Finally, he looked Tonya in the eye, and though she returned his gaze, he couldn't decipher her expression. It disturbed him a great deal, for she wore the same expression she always wore when he talked to her about these things in private, but until now, he'd always assumed that, in the general sense, she agreed with him. It was the same moon-shaped face, framed with red hair, the same brown eyes, the same half smile, but there was something behind the face that made his dinner go sour in his stomach, and made his face hot. He thought for a moment that he should ask her what was eating her, but her eyes seemed one jot sharper, and one jot clearer than they usually were, and they seemed to say, Go ahead, ask me how I feel? and he decided all he should say was, "You can turn the TV back on or whatever.

151

I'm done." He stood there for another awkward ten seconds or so, and lumbered to the kitchen.

V

black boy

As it turned out, Garret Hooker and Derrick Oates became classmates in Mrs. Velma Wafer's sixth-grade class at Waller Elementary, a small tree- and grass-poor campus just outside the Shreveport city limits. Garret first saw the lanky colored boy at the bus stop on First Street East on the Monday following his father's lecture. The morning was cold and sunny, and the boy stood about ten feet from the small group of regular riders, most of whom Garret had known for a long time. There were the "Bird Girls," Cindy Birdsong and Wendy Byrd, hunched together like a couple of magpies, giggling and whispering in the usual way. Next to the Bird Girls stood Kim and Kyle Spicer, hanging close to each other, but not talking, as usual. There was Tim Long, who'd just moved here from Michigan back in the fall, and he was twirling his glasses in his hand, talking in a loud voice about the Super Bowl with Bobby Target, who was wagging his right hand as though trying to stir up campfire smoke, and saying, "It's obvious, it's obvious, Tim; it's obvious." Ordinarily, Garret would have sidled up to Tim and Bobby in hopes of insinuating himself into their conversation, and if they were feeling generous, they might actually look his way from time to time, and even tolerate him speaking, if he was careful not to say anything stupid. But the safest thing to do, as he planned to do today, was

152

set himself next to the Spicer twins, and coax a few grunts from Kyle.

The colored boy was very tall, very skinny. He wore a dark blue pea coat, and pants that were so short that you could almost see the tops of his ugly light green socks. Already Garret had several reason to hate the boy. First off, he was goofy looking. He had big eyes with girly lashes, small pointy ears, and his glasses sat crooked on his flat nose. He had a prissy mouth that made him look conceited, even though he had absolutely no reason to be. Kind of ugly. Big feet, jacket sleeves too short, hands too big. If he tries anything, I'll kill him. Who does he think he is? He knew his father was right about the boy. He was definitely a thief, but the talk he'd had with his mother, last night, about some of the other things his father had said, lingered in his mind.

She came to his room almost every night to tuck him in, to talk to him about anything that was on her mind, or his. When he was little, she would read to him, sing songs to him, tickle his ribs, but in the last couple years she would just talk. He loved it. He couldn't imagine saying to her what his brothers had said: that they were getting too old for night talk, songs and stories, silly word games. How could they sleep without all those stories about the Indians in South Dakota, or the stories about her childhood? Junior and Devon would tease him about what they called "Tinkerbell Time with Mom," but their real reason for riding him was probably because it was so obvious to them that Mommy favored him. So what if it was because he was the youngest, and because he had asthma? So what if he cried more than the others? So what? He had his own room, which was right next to Mom and Dad's; she almost never let Dad spank him, and he had fewer chores than the other two. Besides keeping his room clean, all he had to do was clear the table after dinner, and that was okay, because Mom always sneaked him extra dessert that he could eat in the kitchen while she did the dishes.

When she came into his room last night, his mind was still hot from the things his father had said. His father's mood and words, his nervousness made Garret almost sick with anxiety. They were right next door, a family of thieves. They would probably play loud soul music, and eat with their hands. Be cool if it was Gene Washington or Bob Hayes, so we could get free tickets, prob'ly, to the Cowboys games, but this is different. These are bad people. Dangerous. His mind tumbled with images of unprovoked attacks on his mother, himself, his brothers. The colored mother throws a pot of boiling soup in Mom's face when Mom goes to welcome them. The colored father stabs Dad in the back with a stiletto while Dad's leaning over the engine of the Chrysler. His bike is missing. Devon's bike is missing. Junior's bike is missing. The cat is dead; they've cut his throat, and left him on the front stoop. The colored boy steals one of their cars, takes it for a joyride, crashes it into a house where a baby is sleeping, and he kills the baby. The boy doesn't care. He just laughs as the baby's mother screams, and he runs off into the night. Garret's brow grew fevered from these thoughts, and he was never happier to see his mother as she stepped into his room last night.

She wore her long nightgown, the one with the pink roses all over it, and Dad's old blue robe, which she wore more often than he did. Long ravels hung all over the robe, and it was completely worn through at the elbows. She pulled at the ravels as she spoke, but she never broke them off. She pulled at them the way she gently tugged at Corky's coat when she took the flea comb to him. And her voice seemed the same way, too, a gentle pulling sound—he had no other words for it—that drew every tension from his mind and body, leaving him slack and grateful. But last night she was more serious than most other nights, and she held her voice to whispers, mostly. She seemed almost grave when she began by saying, "Your father's a very wise man, Sonny, but your father's wisdom is only part of the things you'll learn in life. A lot of things go into a person while growing up. It's like with the flowers in my garden, see? They couldn't very well grow in soil without water, or water without soil. They need all sorts of things to grow, like sunshine, soil, rain, even wind.

"You've got to feed on everything that comes your way— the good things, that is—so you can be strong and fit for anything life brings you. You just can't go to one person, or one book for all the wisdom you'll need for a lifetime. You can't read the Bible to learn how to grow crops, or fix a car engine. And I can teach you anything you want to know about archery, or skiing, or cooking, or gardening, but you'll have to talk to Daddy about mechanics or bowling. If you could learn about life from only one thing, or book, or person, you'd have no need for your own thoughts and feelings. We'd all be machines, waiting to be filled up with the same parts.

"Daddy's father was a very wise man, but Daddy and Grampa always disagreed about things. Oh, God, you should have heard those two. They argued about sports and food, and money, cars. Cars! The things they said about cars. You'd think they were deciding the fate of the galaxy." She rolled a few ravel ends together, then smoothed the little braid against her thigh. Then she placed her hand on his knee, and said, "My point is, Sonny, is that everybody has different ideas

155

about what life is about, 'cause every life is different. Now, I don't know all that much about Negro life because I grew up in a place where you almost never saw Negroes. Your father's life was different from mine, and so his ideas are different. Your father went through more hard times before he was twenty than most people have for their entire lives. Both his parents were drinkers; they divorced when he was younger than you are now. His sisters left his home in Baltimore before he turned eighteen, and he has no idea, to this day, what they do, where they live, exactly. You see, already you can see how different your childhood is from how his was. We all have different things to learn in life, and have to make up our own minds about it all.

"All those things he says about his childhood in Baltimore are true, as far as I know. He's never said a lot about it, but he did tell me once about this big boy named Camby, a colored boy, who used to pick on him. Camby used to follow him home from school every day, for months, and make him go into his house and bring something for Camby to eat. It had to be something Camby liked, always some kind of meat. And your father's family was poor and meat was hard to come by until your grandmother remarried. She married a butcher, you see. But anyway, if Camby didn't like what your dad would bring him, Camby would beat him with a leather belt, just like a father does a son. As a matter of fact, Camby used to say he used the belt on all the boys who didn't have fathers—"

Garret lifted his head. "But he had a father," he said. "Grampa was his father."

"Of course he did, but Grampa lived hundreds of miles away, up in Massachusetts, and I'm sure Camby didn't know that, and I'm sure he didn't care. Camby used to tell your father, 'I'm your daddy now, boy, and you'll do as I say.' Isn't that awful? It just must have been terrible—"

"Because your real dad spanks you because he loves you, but—"

"Yes, yes, that's true, son, but well . . . your father had to put up with this Camby boy until Camby was sent to juvenile hall for doing something terrible to his own sister—"

"Like what? What'd he do?"

"He beat her or something. I don't know, but my point is that in spite of all the things your father's learned in his own life, you're responsible for finding out about things on your own. You should listen carefully to everything he says because he is so wise, but . . . You know, if I'd listened to everything that your father said about Negroes, Mrs. Brophie and I never would have become friends, and I wouldn't have had so many nice memories to take with me from our time in England. Daddy won't admit it, but he liked the Brophies very much, and he told me that Sergeant Brophie reminded him of his best friend in Baltimore in his last year in high school, this colored fellow named Dennis Tansimore, who wrote your father every Christmas until just before you were born. Then they just stopped writing."

She folded her arms, looked up at the ceiling, then straight into Garret's eyes. "Well, your father just stopped writing him back," she said, and then she paused. "He used to talk about him all the time before Daddy and I married, but . . ." She let her words fade, and she looked away from him, and at a poster of Don Meredith throwing a long bomb against the Chiefs. She stared at it for such a long time that Garret found himself growing uncomfortable. He thought she might start crying, and he sat up in bed so he could hug her, if she needed him to.

Then abruptly she turned to him, and he saw that she had been crying, a little, but it didn't seem she needed a hug. She said, "Sonny, I want you to promise me one thing. Can you do Mommy this one favor?" And of course he said that he would. "Son, I just want us to always talk. No matter what, I want us to always talk. I mean, if I ever do something that you don't like and it makes you mad as the dickens, I want you to talk to me, and tell me how you feel, instead of keeping it all from me, so I'll never know what happened or what I did to offend you. And I promise I'll always do the same thing for you. There's nothing in the world that you can do that will ever make me stop talking to you. Do you know that?"

He'd never thought about it before, but he said he knew, and then she kissed him on the forehead three times, as she did every night, stood, turned out the light and closed his door behind him. In no time, he was asleep. She woke him at six-thirty, he dressed, ate and left the house, crossed the street, stood on the corner, just a dozen feet from the boy who lived next door. All he knew about him was that he had tried to steal his father's car last night. He knew that if he couldn't beat him up, Devon or Junior could, most likely. All the boy had to do was start something, and that would be it. He'd be sorry he ever came to Barksdale Air Force Base.

At five after seven, the bus pulled up, and, as they did every day, the kids rushed to the door, and crowded on, except for the new boy, who waited till everybody was on before he climbed the steps and found a seat. Garret held his breath until the boy passed his seat, and sat somewhere in the back where he wouldn't have to look at him.

v i

dean's foot

Five peculiar things happened on Derrick's first school day. The first peculiar thing was the cut on Dean's foot. As Derrick arose from sleep, he discovered his brother sitting on his bed, pressing a towel to his foot. Dean's forehead and upper lip glistened with perspiration, and his eyes were closed. Before Derrick could ask his brother what he was doing, his mother shot into the room and sat next to Dean. She carried ice enfolded in a hand towel in her right hand and wrapped her left arm around Dean's shoulders. She rested the ice pack on her knees. "Does it still hurt, Punkin?" she said, as she gently pushed Dean's hand away from the sole of his foot. Dean winced. Dark blood rolled from the wound. "Not really," Dean said.

"Jeez," said Derrick, "what happened to you?"

"Stepped on *some*thing," said Dean.

"Glass? Did you break something?"

Portia pressed the ice pack against Dean's foot, and without looking up she said, "Get ready for school, boy."

"Yes, ma'am. What did he step on?"

"I think it—"

"Boy, what did I say?"

"Get ready for school."

"Then do as I say!"

As Derrick turned to make his bed he sighed, and immediately his mother shoved him onto his bed with her foot. She flew at him as he rolled over and she pinned him onto the bed, tightly gripping his upper arms. "You think you grown, boy? You think it's fine to blow your breath and roll your eyes at me? I don't care how big you get, I'm your mother. I'm your mother even when you turn ninety-five. Do you understand me, nigger?"

"Yes, ma'am! Yes, ma'am!"

"Well, it's good you do, 'cause, if you wanna live on your own, you *know* where the door is. Now get your ass up and get ready for school." Portia released him, returned to Dean's side and took over pressing the ice pack against his foot. Derrick made his bed, dressed in the clothes his mother had laid out for him last night, and went to the bathroom to brush his teeth. There in the bathroom, he inspected the floor for broken glass, but found none. He sighed, and the image of his mother's angry face swept so quickly through his mind that he didn't catch it; it didn't register in emotion, but in a chill along his arms and up to his throat. His anger was so deep in him he didn't feel it, would never have admitted to it if he'd been accused of it. He thought of Dean's foot, believed the tremor in his arms was his concern for his brother, and his horror at the speed and thickness of Dean's blood. The blood made him think of the things John Powers had said.

He walked to the living room, rather than the kitchen, in hopes of finding his sister, whom he hoped to speak to. For the whole weekend, she had had to stay as close to their mother as a handmaiden, and hadn't been able to talk. Alva was in high school, and was to catch her bus a half an hour earlier than Derrick and Dean. Lately, she seemed to be more in the corner of his eyes than in full view, but in Derrick's mind, the reasons for her elusiveness had to do with something more than the scurry of moving. From the time Sergeant Oates received orders for Barksdale, Alva grew more distant from Derrick and their father, but closer to their mother and Dean. She took Dean to the library now, rather than Derrick, and accompanied their mother on almost all her errands. Portia and Alva could often be heard speaking in soft, low notes from behind the closed door of Alva's room. He sometimes believed they were talking about him, though he couldn't have said why. Alva and Portia watched soaps together, when they could, and when Alva couldn't watch, Portia recounted every plot from every show they followed over morning coffee. She rarely had anything at all to say to Derrick these days, except to point out some inaccuracy in his speech, or his accounts of his school studies. This dismayed Derrick, but he couldn't imagine speaking to Alva about it, even though he was fairly sure he'd done or said something to offend her. He hoped things would get better.

Alva sat on the couch, watching the *Today* show and absently pulling at the buttons of her plaid dress. He took it that she was aware of Dean's foot because the grim set of her face had nothing to do with the jolly weather report the man on TV was giving. Derrick sat on the couch, allowing one full cushion between them. "Did you see what happened to Dean's foot?" said Derrick.

"I don't see how you could have slept through all the noise he made. Of course I saw it. I got to him before Mama did."

"What'd he step on?"

"He doesn't know. We couldn't find anything."

Derrick slowly nodded, considered whether it would be too soon to ask her about the things John Powers had said. On the television there was a commercial for Fab laundry detergent, Jif peanut butter, and the Playtex Living Bra. Alva fingered the collar of her turtleneck, smoothed the pleats of her dress and looked at the clock behind the couch. "Hey, Al," said Derrick, "do you like it here? I mean, so far."

"No."

"Me neither. I wish we could go back to Colorado. Do you like Texas more, or Colorado more?"

"I liked California the best."

"Me, too."

For the first time this morning, she looked at him. "Well why do you wish we were back in Colorado?"

Derrick felt himself blush. He folded his arms over his chest and sighed. "Al, are you mad at me?" he said.

"No."

"You act like you are."

Alva screwed up her mouth in the way she did when chewing on the inside of it. Again she tugged at the collar of her turtleneck; again she smoothed the pleats of her dress. "I hate it here, that's all. It's not you. I miss Dwayne, and Debbie, and I—"

"I thought you didn't like Dwayne all that much."

"He was my boyfriend!"

"Yeah, but—"

"He was a jerk sometimes; I admit it, but when you're older, you'll understand how complicated these things can be. Listen, shouldn't you be getting ready for school?"

"I'm ready." Derrick felt nervousness course through every limb of his body, and he stretched his arms and legs forward, catlike. He was determined to warn her, even if she didn't like him anymore. He refolded his arms, and said in a rush of words, "I just thought I'd tell you, John Powers said the people here hate colored people. He said they lynch

162

colored people here. He said colored people don't have rights in the southern part of the country—"

Alva spread her arms, and laughed, "Rick, Rick, Rick, we were living in the South in Texas." Alva made her eyes big. Her expression was both wry and exasperated. "Where do you think we were living, Canada?"

" 'Deep South.' John said the Deep South is where we are now."

"What's the difference? What's the difference, Rick? Louisiana couldn't be any less redneck than Texas was, and besides, can you think of one place where we ever lived where there was no prejudice? You remember when we were driving through Waco and those boys tried to run us off the road? You remember when our house got egged last year? Who else's house was egged? Who else had their bikes taken apart and had the parts tossed all over the backyard? You remember how I wasn't even allowed to try out for cheerleader, and how they practically drafted Debbie? You remember the boy who had firecrackers thrown at him on the way from the bus stop? Well I hope you do, 'cause it was you, Rick. What's the difference between Texas rednecks and Louisiana rednecks?"

"Listen, little brother, John Powers was just trying to scare you. No one's lynching anyone here or anywhere else. He was exaggerating. They used to do that kind of thing, I guess, but not anymore. Just ask Mom or Dad, if you don't believe me, which you never do.

"And by the way, hasn't anyone ever told you that we don't use 'colored' anymore. It's Afro-American or Black. I prefer Black."

Before Derrick could give any kind of answer, Sergeant

163

Oates, dressed in his fatigues, cap, coat and boots, stepped into the house, and said to Alva, "Are they ready to go?"

Alva looked at Derrick, and said, "Was Dean dressed?" but again, before he could answer, their father slipped down the hallway, and in a moment, returned carrying Dean in his arms. Dean had a tourniquet round his leg, above the knee, and cotton bandages wrapped around his foot. He was smiling. "See you guys later," he said, and he waved. Portia followed Anton and Dean out the door, repeating the things someone at the hospital had told her about how Dean should be handled on the way there. "We got it, Portia; we can handle it, right, Bud?" Dean gave a quick thumbs-up, and Portia shut the door. "School, young lady; breakfast, young man," she said, then went into the kitchen.

The second peculiar thing happened at breakfast. As his mother told him that he would have to check himself into the school this morning, she set out for him a bowl of cereal, a cup of milk, and a glass of Tang. "I've already called the school about your brother," she said. "The secretary is supposed to meet you when you get off the bus. Just find the lady in the tan coat and blue skirt." She moved to the sink and turned on the taps. Derrick saw that the Tang sat at the bottom of the glass unstirred, so he stirred it and drank a third of it in one draft. He then poured the milk over the cereal, and when he did so, a large cockroach crawled out from under several flakes, rested on the lip of the bowl and began cleaning itself. "Mama, there's a roach in my cereal," Derrick said, and pointed at it with the spoon. His mother turned from the sink, and said, "Well, son, there's a whole lot of roaches in this lousy state, so you might as well get used to them." She plucked Derrick's spoon from his hand, and looked at the roach. "He's a bold rascal," she said, "and big, too." She flicked the roach onto the floor and coolly crushed it under her foot. She said, "When we were stationed in Laredo, before you were born, I found a scorpion in the kitchen cabinet." She went to the utility closet, removed a broom, and as she swept the roach out the back door, she said, "I was so scared, your father had to kill it for me." She laughed. "I kept the cabinet taped shut all day till he got home from work." She shut the back door and said, "Now hurry up and eat so you don't miss your bus, darlin.'"

The third thing was that Derrick got the second highest grade on the spelling test that Mrs. Wafer administered that day. Ordinarily, Derrick was a terrible speller, something his parents found both frustrating and baffling, given the fact that his teachers considered him bright, and that he was an avid reader. Mrs. Wafer told him he could take the test "just for fun," since he was new and hadn't studied any of the words.

He was unsure what to think of Velma Wafer. She seemed cordial enough when she welcomed him to the class, but she kept mispronouncing his name, or calling him by the wrong name. Several times she called him Daryl, which sounded like "Durl" because of her accent. He was far too meek to correct her, but sometime during the course of the day, she discovered her error, and without apologizing for it or admitting her mistake in any way, began to call him by his right name, which sounded more like Dirk to his ears. She wasn't a handsome woman, and perhaps because of this, he thought she might carry a sizable mean streak. She carried her tall, thin body stiffly, and her face was round and jowly, as though it belonged to a plump woman of short stature. The thick lenses of her bifocals made her eyes appear far too small, and the frames weren't large enough to obscure the pea-sized wart beneath her left eye. To Derrick, one of the most unpleasant things about her was her breath, a mixture of tobacco, Listerine, and something that reminded Derrick of pickles. He could smell it whenever she came within two or three feet of him. But the thing that bothered him the most was her insinuation that Derrick didn't belong at Waller, but at Washington Elementary, an all-black school in Shreveport.

Derrick knew, from overhearing his parents, that the majority of the black families on base sent their children to the all-black schools in town. But they wanted to send their children to what they believed to be the better schools, and besides, those who chose to send their children to the black schools had to provide their own transportation and the Oates family had only one car, which Sergeant Oates drove to work. Derrick was very accustomed to being the only black child in his classes, or one of two or three. At the moment he was too nervous about being stared at by every student in his class, and hardly gave a thought to his "racial" difference from the rest of them. He wouldn't have thought of it for perhaps the entire day had not Mrs. Wafer said to him, "Well, I hope you'll be happy here, Dirk, but if not, I'm sure they'd love to have you at Washington. No doubt you'd be more comfortable, too. Tell me, did Mother and Daddy take you into town so you could get a look at that school?"

"No ma'am."

"Well, I'm sure we'll enjoy having you here." She assigned him a seat, and when the class settled a bit, she began the test.

Derrick earned a 95. Mrs. Wafer announced it to the class, and they buzzed as excitedly as if she'd handed out money. Derrick assumed Mrs. Wafer had miscalculated his grade, and would correct it soon.

The fourth peculiar thing happened, somewhat, as a result of the third. After the exam, Mrs. Wafer dismissed them for recess. Four boys practically hung to Derrick as he left the room, and followed him out to the bare dirt playground. The weather had warmed to something in the high sixties, and few students wore their jackets or coats. Only one boy of the four who followed Derrick wore a jacket, an exceedingly pale, black-haired, freckled boy, with puffy eyelids. The boy kept touching Derrick's elbow, stepping on his heels. "Say, boy, what's your name, Durril or Durrick?" the boy said. Derrick walked to the center of the playground and stood beneath a tall elm tree.

"Derrick."

"So how come you're so smart?" said the boy who'd asked him the first question. Two boys stood behind the black-haired boy, and the fourth one stood next to Derrick, as though he and Derrick were well acquainted. He was standing too close, so Derrick moved a little to his left. "I'm not so smart. It was an easy test."

"Well I only got a sixty-five on it."

"I got a sixty," said one of the boys next to the black-haired boy.

"I guess I got lucky," Derrick said. There followed a long and awkward silence. "What's your name?" said Derrick. The boy said his name was Stanley, and he introduced the two beside him, but Derrick couldn't catch their names. The fourth boy had apparently gone away.

"Where you from?" Stanley said.

"Allover, USA."

"Oliver? Where's that?"

Stanley stood directly in front of him, and much too close. His mouth was set in a half smile–half sneer and he squinted ironically at Derrick, his arms folded over his chest. Stanley looked at the ground, then back up at Derrick and stepped closer to him. "I'm from Colorado," said Derrick.

"Well, where's that?"

Derrick grinned at the boy, assumed he was joking, but when Stanley didn't return his smile, Derrick said, "It's north of Texas, west of Kansas, and south of—" Suddenly, the boy pushed him, not violently, but not exactly playfully either. Derrick had no idea what to make of it, so he grinned again, and said, "What'd you do that for?" Stanley answered by pushing him again. "You're pretty smart, aren't you, Colorada?" He pushed Derrick a third time, hard enough to cause Derrick to take a backward step, which resulted in Derrick's stepping on the hand of the boy whom he thought had left their group. That boy had moved, by degrees, from beside Derrick to behind him, and then he had gotten down on his hands and knees to facilitate Stanley's knocking Derrick onto his back. This was something Derrick had only seen the Three Stooges or the Marx Brothers do, and he had no idea what to make of it. When Derrick stepped on the hand of the boy behind him, he said, "Excuse me," then, when he realized what was happening, said, "Oh, I see," and he smiled again. "*That's* why you were pushing me." The boy who'd been crouching stood up, dusted off the knees of his jeans. The other three boys grinned and blushed. Stanley said, "We done it wrong, huh?"

"Yeah, I guess."

They all burst into a subdued laughter, as though someone had told a mildly funny dirty joke, and Stanley offered his hand and Derrick clasped it, shook it. Derrick was as embarrassed as the others. "We'll get you next time," the boy said, and gave Derrick a friendly clap on the shoulder.

Derrick said, "Okay," and shrugged, but he had no idea whether the whole thing was in jest, or in earnest. The teacher on the playground blew her whistle, signaling the end of recess.

Derrick noticed the fifth thing by stages. For most of the day he was no more aware of it than one would be of a three-degree rise in room temperature. One's body may sense it in every respect, but it wouldn't necessarily register in one's conscious thoughts. But slowly, degree by degree, Derrick began to notice that the stocky redhead sitting one row over and one seat behind him was staring at him with the intensity of a heat lamp. The heat of the stare reached his consciousness sometime during lunch, but when it did reach the point of consciousness, he understood that it had gone on for the whole of the day, and that he would feel it for the remainder of the day. He believed that there was hatred in the boy's glare, though only once did he find the nerve to turn in his seat and look directly at him. And when he did, he was so concerned about drawing Mrs. Wafer's attention, that he couldn't really focus on the redhead. Nevertheless, he perceived the boy's stare, as if through his skin. He felt it prickling the back of his neck, grazing his left cheek, burning the collar of his shirt like a beam of light through a magnifying glass.

It was darker in its feel than Dean's blood, more unnerving than a roach in a cereal bowl, more inexplicable than his correctly spelling "precaution," "temporary," "vestibule," "incinerate," more awkward and ineffable than the aborted encounter with Stanley and his friends. He wanted to fly from his seat and throw himself at the boy, pluck out those staring eyes with his thumbs. He wanted to scream. He saw himself plunging his pencil into the boy's eyes. He wanted to vanish into the air. He wanted to turn around in his seat once more, and stare hard enough in return to melt the boy's flesh, turn his clothes to ash. He wanted the day to end. He wanted to go home and eat flavorless food, watch television through closed lids, bathe in water so tepid it had no feel, sleep and dream everything in black.

But when the bell rang, and it *was* time to go home, the stocky redhead boarded Derrick's bus, got off at the very same stop, entered the quarters that was contiguous to his own, so all through the night the boy's gaze cut through the walls, knocked over furniture, filled his room with a red heat that wouldn't cool. It wouldn't stop. Before he shut out the lights at bedtime, he wanted to tell Dean about his peculiar day, but somehow he couldn't. The only conversation he could manage dealt with Dean's day at the hospital and at home. He asked Dean, "Hey, did you ever find out what you stepped on this morning?"

Dean said, "Nope. I looked all day for something that could have done it, but I couldn't find a thing."

vii

car wash

On the first Saturday after the second week of school, Sergeant Hooker sent Garret, Devon and Junior outside to wash the Rambler wagon and the Chrysler. He stood at the open front door, smoking, supervising. They moved around and through each car like a pit crew. They really didn't need watching over, but it was a beautiful, quiet midmorning, and there was little else to do. He spent more time watching the smoke curl away from his cigarette or the clouds overhead change shape than he did the boys. Today was the first warm, sunny day in a month, and he knew they were grateful to be out, even if it meant doing chores. They had been suffering from cabin fever since this unusually cold January had rolled in. They'd grown accustomed to the weather here, now, but in their first couple of years, English fat lay beneath their skin, and the summers were unbearable, the winters sublime. Now the opposite felt true. From January to March, winter felt like winter again. The boys tended to stay indoors and watch television, or build models. Their minds grew frowsty—as the old Limes used to say—with all the glue-breathing and TV glow. He sent them out whenever he could, to shag flies or fling the pigskin, but it didn't seem worth it because of Tonya's carping about how they were ruining their clothes in that goddamned muddy field. Besides, the field was adjacent to Sergeant Oates's yard, and their oldest boy inhabited the field like a squatter. He was always there, poking that round, serious face into his boys' huddles, or slipping his hands into his boys' mitts. Why can't

he stroll his lanky ass up First Street East and play with those
niggers up on Pelican? Four blocks and he could be with his
own kind. But no, he had the kind of "Negro" parents who
need to prove they can keep up with the white man. Bet they
like it when he plays with our boys.

Figures, what with Oates being so yellow and his woman
being so pretty. They got the kinds of colored faces whites
don't mind seeing, and they're quiet as Japs. They want their
boys to sneak up, mix in, lighten up the herd a bit, I guess.
They're like your shadow, always there, even in the dark. You
get used to them, in a way. You start thinking they're just like
everyone else. But they're not. Just go up on Pelican, go live in
Baltimore. That'll educate you. They're drawn to us like moths
to light. Moths to fucking light. Never understand what Ma
thought she was doing. Drawn to them, easy with them, talked
like them, after a while, like it was her first language. "Ma, why
you talking like that? What's with this 'Lord-a-mercy' stuff?
And how come we eat like we do now, with all these pig parts
and stuff. Why can't we go home? What are we doing here?"
She'd always say, "We are home. This is home. I was born
here. My sister lives five minutes from here; your grandparents
died here. You wanna go home? Close your eyes and tap your
heels together three times, then open 'em and see where
you are."

Hooker heard one of his boys curse, and he looked up from
the cigarette in his right hand in time to see Garret sling his
chamois right into Junior's face. Hooker was off the stoop and
clasping Junior about the waist before the boy could retaliate.
Junior was big, at least one hundred eighty pounds, and it
wouldn't be long before he'd be shrugging off whippings like
raindrops. "Whoa, whoa, whoa, there, young man, what the

hell are you—Garret! What the hell'd you do that for? Have you lost your nut?"

"He said Derrick was my girlfriend."

Junior giggled. "I said he was your boyfriend . . . ya pud."

Devon said, "Hey, if he prefers girlfriend, let it be girlfriend." Devon twisted the water hose shut and dropped it on the grass. "Yeah, Dad, he's always staring at Derrick. He acts like he's in love with him."

"I do not!"

"He does," said Junior, as his father released him. "And he's always *talking* about him."

"Because I *don't* like him, not because I do."

Garret appeared to be on the verge of bawling, and if he does, thought Hooker, I'll burn his ass, then ground him for two weeks no matter what Tonya says. I won't raise no sissy. "Calm yourself, Sonny," he said, then, "Junior, Devon, you guys finish my cars and when you're done, go see what your mother needs help doing. And you, you come with me." He clutched Garret by the shoulder and walked him to the stoop. "Sit with me," he said. He stared at the boy with a look somewhere between disgust and pity. He would have found Garret easier to discipline if he weren't so small, and if he weren't the spitting image of Tonya. And he was a good boy. Always does as he's told, tries hard to please us, smart. "Tell me why you don't like that colored boy, Sonny," said Hooker. "He been bothering you?"

"No, he doesn't bother me. I just don't like him."

"Is it true you been staring at him, talking about him a lot?"

"He's in my class at school."

"And?"

"I don't like him. What's the big deal? He bothers me, Dad."

"You just said—"

"I don't mean he does anything; I'm just saying he annoys me. Yeah, annoys, just by being around. He always wants to play with us, and he does the same thing at school."

"Wants to play with you at school, too, huh?"

"Yeah."

Hooker looked carefully at the boy, at the way he dipped his head, the way his cheeks burned twice as crimson when he'd mentioned school. Staring at him all the time, talking about him all the time. He could see what was going on, and he saw how to ferret it out. This would be easy. "Tell me something else, Sonny. How do the other fellas at school feel about Sergeant Oates's boy? They get annoyed at him like you do?"

"They don't like him, but they let him play football and hang around sometimes. I don't see why, 'cause he's not so good at it, and he's weird. He talks about weird stuff, riots and stuff. And how to hang guys, and cut 'em up and stuff. Stanley Dumonde and some of the guys said they were supposed to fight him, but so far they haven't done anything. Stanley says he's a communist."

"A communist!"

"That's what Stan says. 'Cause one day he brung this book from the base library—"

"Who did?"

"Derrick Oates did. He brung a book that had this picture in it of this dead colored guy hanging from a tree. He only wanted to show me, but some of the other guys came over 'cause they thought we were looking at dirty pictures, but—"

"A dead colored fella?"

"Uh-huh. There were all these people standing around, smiling and pointing up to him—in the picture?—and the colored

174

guy's head was all cocked to the side, and he did look pretty dead, but I think it was from a movie or something, because—"

"From the *base* library?"

"Yuh-huh, but I didn't think it was real 'cause one of the white men's eyes were shiny like when you see a cat at night, and Michael Trudeaux said people's eyes can't do that, and Stanley said he didn't think the colored guy's eyes were closed all the way—"

"You're telling me he got such a book from the *base* library."

"Yuh-huh. His sister checked it out. To win a bet, I think. Derrick said it was real. It did look pretty real, and I couldn't sleep good for two nights after he showed it to me. Derrick said white people used to hang colored people like that all the time, but he doesn't know if they still do. Anyway, Mrs. Wafer took it away from him. She said it was in poor taste. After she did, Stanley told me he was trying to start a riot, and we should fisticuff him before he does something else. He could ruin the whole school."

"I'll be darned. Only wanted to show you?"

"I don't know why."

"Um." Hooker threaded his fingers together and squeezed them tight. "Because he likes to annoy you."

"That's what I mean, Dad; he annoys me practically every day."

"But if you and the fellas started some mess with him, you'd all get in trouble, wouldn't you?"

"We *could* get expelled. Especially Stanley, 'cause he's been suspended twice already."

"Idn't that the boy who used to pick on you in fourth grade?"

"And fifth, but he leaves me alone now. All of 'em do. No one bothers me much anymore, since you talked to the principal." Garret lowered his head a bit, and said, "Except they still call me names. Are you gonna talk to the principal about Derrick?"

"Not if he hasn't done anything bad, Sport. But we are entitled to keep to ourselves, aren't we? If he wants to play football around here, he can go up Pelican Street. If he wants to play at school, well, he can go to school with his kind. But I'm pretty fresh out of ideas, son. They're pretty stubborn people, coloreds, and it just won't do to politely ask him to leave you guys be. I'm afraid it'll take something strong. You know, something that'll make him see the light, so to speak. You know what I mean, son?"

"You mean like play a trick on him?"

"Well, sort of. We could make it so he doesn't want to hang around you fellas."

"Like what?"

"When your brothers are done, the three of us'll sit down and hammer things out. I wanna warn you, though. We're probably gonna have to do something strong. We might even have to hurt him some. Can you deal with that, Sonny Boy?"

Garret didn't move or speak for a long enough time for Sergeant Hooker to confirm for himself that Garret was the second person in his family to befriend a nigger, and when the boy did speak there wasn't so much as a penny's worth of conviction. The boy went so pale you could count every one of his freckles, and all he said was, "We could just ignore him. Just not talk to him when he comes around us." Sergeant Hooker's stomach felt hard and cold, and his ears beat with blood. First Tonya, then Sonny. As far as he was concerned, this constituted an epidemic. His mother didn't count, for she no longer existed, and as for himself, well, it was one thing when you went to a school full of them, but something quite different when you could choose. Besides, Dennis Tansimore had been so different from the rest of them. Hell, Dennis got it worse than I did. His goofy limp, his jigaboo fright-wig hair, his love for kites, his stupid model skeletons, his Chinese eyes, his gorilla lips, his ashy elbows and acne. You either had to hate him or love him on sight. Most kids hated him. Hooker himself may have been the only one who treated him decently. What choice did I have? What choice? So fucking lonely and didn't even have a dog. Ma's niggerman allergic to animal hair. And he was there all the damn time. Dogs were out.

Dennis was my dog. I was worse to him than they were, in a way, 'cause I told him I liked him. I never liked him. Mean to him is what I was, but he never seemed to notice, or didn't care. But I never tripped him in the halls, or jammed his head into toilets. Never whipped him like Camby did me. Like Camby did him, too, only not like me. No one ever got it like me. But fuckgoddamnit to fuck, we were all dogs, when you get down to it. Camby, the dog you had to feed. Tansimore, the dog you teased. I was the dog you whipped.

He understood Camby and Tansimore because, like himself, they were extremes of one thing or another: Camby, red and hungry; Tansimore, black and sorrowful; Hooker, pale and mean. Sometimes he missed them because, unlike so much of the world, they were exactly what they appeared to be. He needed men like Camby so he could focus his hate, and men like Tansimore to focus his pity, which he put in the place of love. He believed he couldn't feel love. But I was good to him, just never liked him, is all. What'd we have in common? Nothing. Not a thing. Being whipped by Camby? What was that? That what you build it on? Blood brothers are supposed to choose to bleed themselves, then share it. Nobody's supposed to do it for you.

But they had more in common than being whipped by Camby, it was just that—in the same way Hooker chose to believe his mother dead—he chose not to remember these other things: their broken homes, their love for the Orioles, their hate for the city. They talked about moving away all the time. They'd go to California, where Hooker would become a race care driver; Tansimore, an osteopath. They'd live in the same tree-lined street five minutes from the ocean, five minutes from each other. Dennis would name his first boy Eugene; Eugene would do Dennis the same honor. They daily talked about these things, and they believed in them like they believed in flesh and blood, but when Hooker's mother married the black man, he sealed his heart beneath miles of cold wax, and stone and water, and stopped believing in anything that began or ended with black people. As the years went by, he learned to bury words, too. He would never admit to anyone, not even Tonya, that he'd once really cared for Dennis. He lied to himself about it for years, then forgot he'd lied.

Perhaps he and Dennis Tansimore would still be friends if not for the things Dennis had said about "our heritage" in the last couple of letters he'd received from him. Dennis had gotten weird. Dennis knew how much Mom hurt me, and he still had the nerve to congratulate him. Told him never to talk about my family, and he did. And all those letters about Pan-Africa and Mali, and pyramids and shit. Always had these obsessions.

Skeletons. Paper fucking skeletons. Karate, bebop, Rasputin, Mali. Butterflies. Trains, genetics, kites, animal bones. Animal bones, like he was some kind of voodoo priest. Paper fucking skeletons. I believe he went crazy. Probably thought everybody in the world was a nigger. Motherfucker wrote, "Nothing more beautiful than a black mouth on a white breast, or a white penis held fast in an ebony hand." Sick. "For the good of the world," he said. Fucking sick. "You should marry black," he said. "I will marry white or tan. Our children will be blood brothers and sisters." Nonsense. Fucking sick, sick man. Had to cut him loose. Just had to cut the sumbitch loose. "Sonny," Sergeant Hooker said, "It's too late for all that." He could barely keep himself from spitting out the words, and nearly every time he blinked he thought of slapping the red back into his boy's face. But he had to be calm about this whole thing. "No, son, I'm afraid it's too late for that. Sure, you could ignore him, but he'll have an excuse for acting all hurt, and he'll look at you like you all are just going through a stage, and you'll get over it and be buddies again before long. He'll keep talking to you, asking you to play. No, son, that way'll take months for him to get it through his thick head you really do mean business. No, we need to do something he'll remember for his whole life. Something to let him know we mean business right then, and right there." Hooker placed his hand on Garret's shoulder. "Sonny boy," he said, "are you ready to do something very strong to that boy to teach him his lesson? Are you gonna be a man with me on this?" He could see the boy was worked up, could see he was on the verge of tears, and he could see him trying to breathe deeply, unlock his throat so he could speak in a voice that wouldn't give him away. "Come on, Sonny; don't leave me twisting in the wind. You're gonna be a man for me, aren't you?"

"Okay."

"What's the matter, son? You're not scared, are you?"

"No."

"Well, you look scared. . . . Are you sure?"

"I'm sure."

"You sick?"

"No."

"You're all pale, little man. Look at your hands shake."

"Daddy?"

"Yes, son."

"I'm—"

"Go on."

". . . fine. I'm fine. You're just . . . I'm just—"

"Something sure seems wrong with you, fella. Hey now, be honest with me. You don't like Sergeant Oates's boy like Devon says, do you?"

"No, Dad."

"I didn't think so. I didn't think so. You're my smartest boy." When Hooker lifted his hand from his shoulder, Garret leapt as if something had slithered beneath his legs. Hooker cupped his hand around his mouth. "Junior! Quit wasting water. You boys get in the house and see what your mom needs." He looked down at Garret. "You too," he said, "after all, you practically started this whole thing. You guys are being punished."

He watched the boys clamber into the house, but heard no one call for Tonya. He assumed they'd gone straight to their rooms. It was hardly worth getting upset about. For one thing, they'd done a great job on the cars. For another, he just wasn't in the mood. For another, he'd done what he'd needed. He was sure everything would be okay, from here on out.

viii

maps

That very same Saturday Portia Oates spent an hour going over a Rand-McNally map of Shreveport–Bossier City with her husband. She was nervous about driving alone in towns she didn't know, and usually she refused to, but Anton would be busy for the next few weekends studying for a senior NCO exam, and had no time to escort her, and both she and Alva needed underwear, and Alva needed shoes. Portia and Alva had already been to the base exchange, but returned home without a thing. "It's the most piss-poor B.X. I've ever seen," Portia had told Anton. "Sorriest bunch of shoes I've ever seen. All that maroon and blue. Who wears maroon and navy pumps anymore? And they must have fifty thousand pairs of size sevens, but one piddly pair of nines in the style Alva looks good in. Wrong color, of course."

"I hate the clothes," Alva had said. "Shifts, muumuus, knee socks, pedal pushers, Capri pants, saddle shoes, Mary Janes."

"Like stepping right back to 1963," said Portia, "all that plaid—"

"No madras, no paisley, and about a million shirtwaist dresses—"

"They had some cute ones."

"I know, Mama, but at least they could've had some with Nehru collars."

"That's true," Portia said, with little conviction. She didn't fully approve of all the current fashions that teenage girls were wearing these days, but she did want Alva to wear clothes that were reasonably appropriate for the times. Granny dresses

might be all right, and bell-bottoms were fine for the weekends, but hip-huggers were positively out, as were miniskirts,
poor-boy shirts, polka dots, and anything too loud. Colors
were getting so loud these days. And color combinations dis-
turbing. Orange and blue? Spring green and scarlet? And
most of the shoes were uglyish, as she would say. She hadn't
made up her mind about the go-go boots that Alva wanted,
but some of those fashions, wedges, high-heeled sandals and
such, seemed a little on the sluttish side. Portia incrementally
shifted their critique from clothing to the base exchange in
general, their small appliances, their music selection, their
linens and dishes, everything seemed selected by someone with
nothing but contempt for military people. But when Anton
suggested that she go into town, she fell silent for a moment
and looked at him as though he were joking. "Honey, I don't
wanna go shopping in all those back-of-the-bus places. And
you know how easily I get lost." Anton shrugged, and said,
"Better'n walking in bad shoes," and went to the hall closet for
the maps.

They sat down at the kitchen table with the map, some
paper and a pen, and at about the time Portia felt resigned to
the fact that she was actually going to do this, to make this
drive, the doorbell rang. Alva went to answer it, and came
back with Mrs. Hooker a half step behind her. Mrs. Hooker
carried a freshly baked coffee cake. "Hi," she said, "I guess
I'm the welcome wagon."

Portia said, "I really want to thank you for helping us like this,
Tonya. I don't think I could have driven on this highway. Look
at how these people drive."

"They are lead footed," Tonya said.

Alva said, "Mrs. Hooker, is it true you can drive at twelve here?"

Portia's stomach clenched every time Tonya turned to address Alva. When her head rolled right, so did the car, and twice they dipped onto the shoulder, and trucks and cars would blast past them, honking. She drove as fast as Anton, but without the control. She spent far too much time pointing at scenery, telling little stories about buildings and people Portia couldn't have cared less about. "Actually," Tonya said, "it's thirteen, but you can get a learner's permit at twelve and six or nine months. I don't remember which. We've got two boys old enough to drive, but our rule is no drivers under sixteen, so Eugene Junior is the only one with a license."

"You have three boys, don't you?" said Portia.

"Uh-huh, but on weekends it feels like thirty."

Portia laughed. "I know what you mean," she said. "My Alva isn't much trouble, but the boys drive me crazy half the time. My oldest boy's *always* on restriction."

"Is he trouble?"

"Nothing serious, just never pays attention."

"I hope he's not on restriction now, 'cause my husband and boys would like to take him fishing next weekend."

"Ricky?"

"He's Garret's classmate—Garret's my youngest, the chubby little carrottop—and they've become friends. Didn't he tell you?"

He never tells me anything, thought Portia, acts like I don't exist. "He's quiet about school," she said.

"He's a very sweet boy. And smart, too, Garret says."

"Well, he's bright, but lazy."

"Oh, I'm sorry, Portia. I guess I'm giving you the impression that Derrick already knows about the fishing trip. Actually, Eugene sent me over to introduce us and ask if your son would like to go. Eugene and the boys just discussed it this morning. They haven't been this excited about anything. Eugene must have reminded me three times to ask you right away, but I just forgot. Usually, he's not . . . he's shy, but I think he's happy that Garret has finally found a good friend. Anyway, I meant to ask, but we got so carried away with talking about the weather and the B.X. and everything, it just slipped my mind."

Portia felt uneasy with this woman, and she couldn't say why. She seemed perfectly nice, nicer than most, and perhaps that was the problem. In her eighteen years as a military wife, no one had ever welcomed her at all to their new quarters, let alone with a coffee cake. Maybe it was just too much relative to what she was used to, and maybe because it happened in the last of all possible places she'd expect. Maybe Tonya hadn't lived here long enough for the South to soak in, but Portia believed in the possibility. She knew white people could so easily, so mindlessly take on the color of whatever forest they lived in. A woman might be your best friend in New York, but run into her nine years later in, say, Tennessee, and you'd swear she'd come up from the very soil of the place. Like that Evelyn Pelham, back-stabbing heifer. Right there in church and she acted like she'd never seen me in her life. Gonna grin at me from behind that nasty pink lipstick and swear she didn't recognize me. "Oh, it's you, Portia. Well, small blue world, idn't it?" Shoulda given her a small blue eye, is what.

But she had learned in these eighteen years that they weren't all the same. While it was true that white people could

184

change accents as easily as one could change shoes, she'd made some good friends over the years. Ginny Weatherford, Willa Tardy, Mary Sue Polland, all fine women with whom she still kept in touch. She looked at Tonya's pretty triangle doll face, her open brown eyes, her freckles, and she thought, I've always had good luck with redheads. Maybe it's because they get teased so much they know a tiny bit about what we go through. Anyone can see this girl's nice. Cute as a button, too.

Although Portia didn't at first know it, what lay beneath her discomfort was that the conversation was about Derrick. If it had been about Alva's being invited to go to a slumber party, or Dean's being asked to ride bikes with the neighborhood boys, she wouldn't have been so disturbed. Alva was usually gregarious and popular. Nearly everyone liked her. Dean was silent as winter, but had charisma, and was good at sports. But Derrick? Always hunched over and prissy mouthed. Always staring with those big eyes, like some kind of hoot owl. No one's ever invited him to parties, and the like, and he's never seemed to care, or even notice. Boy's like a ghost. Settles into rooms like heat, and leaves the same way. Always sneaking, creeping. Who would notice him? Like to give me a stroke when I look up and see him there. A boy should sound like a herd of bison when he walks into the room. Like Dean. Dean sounds like he threw away the shoes and wore the boxes. You couldn't ask for two more different sons. One a little man, the other a ghost boy, a sleepwalker who won't snap out of it no matter how hard you smack him. He'll wind up dead if he don't wake up someday.

"Well, even if he did know," said Portia, "I'd be surprised if he did tell me. He's a strange one. If he does go, you make him mind."

Tonya nodded, and reached into her purse, which rested on

the seat between herself and Portia. She took her eyes completely off the road, and car swerved right. "You need help?" said Portia. "Sunglasses," said Tonya. "The glare is terrible on this road this time of the afternoon." Portia saw the glasses, plucked them out and handed them to the woman. She looked up in time to see the corrugated roof of some laundromat as they reached the crest of a hill. Painted in six-foot letters upon the roof were the words "Whites Only." Alva said, in a voice that lay neatly between innocence and bitterness, "Now what kind of laundromat only does whites?"

Portia was flustered, and said nothing. Tonya edged the glasses up her nose and said, "It's still pretty ugly here, but a girl like you'll make it a whole lot prettier, Alva." Her voice quavered when she spoke, and her face went crab red. She jerked the car straight, and said, "You're lucky to have a girl. I always imagined I'd have at least one. We'd try for another, but I just couldn't handle it if it turned out to be a boy."

"Girls have their own problems. This one smokes."

"I only tried it, Mama."

"So does *my* oldest. Cigarettes, cigars, you name it. Seventeen and smoking like a Corvair."

Portia turned to look at Alva. "Well, from the smell of your clothes, I'd say you're still trying."

"I'm sure they'll get over it, Portia. Anyway, I think you're lucky to have a girl. Shopping would be a whole lot more fun, and appreciated. Men don't notice a thing, but meat, football and boobs."

"I will give you that. Alva's got more good taste in her little finger than my three men have in their whole bodies."

Tonya laughed much harder than the joke warranted, and edged her glasses back up her nose. "Girls are great," she said.

"I'm thankful for my girl," said Portia, and she found her-self wishing that this poor woman would stop trying so hard. Alva's joke had her in a tizzy. It was ridiculous. Tonya acted as though she had been caught by Black Panthers as she stood on the roof with a paintbrush in her hand. Why be guilty? You didn't do anything. And worse than that she acted as though she could explain it all away. She wanted to tell Tonya she knew quite well where she was, and no need to kill yourself to change the subject, girl. She could handle it. It was the kids she worried about. All mothers, she believed, slept only so deep, their anxiety cooled only so much. But as nice as this Tonya woman was, as much as Portia respected her for raising three boys and dealing with the military life, there was nothing so sleep stealing and anxiety heating as raising Negro children in a mostly white world. Every day you had to worry about locals doing harm to your children, and neighbors suspecting harm from them. They watch you all the time, always suspect the worst of you. You have not one idea, girl, how hard it is for us. Do children chase your babies home? Do they egg your house, cut their eyes your way whenever so much as a water sprinkler goes missing from someone's yard? And not only do *you* not understand, but my very own seem not to understand, either. They forget their own brown-skinned selves, and smart off to the wrong people, try to make friends with the wrong people, get hurt because sometimes they are surrounded by the wrong people. It's the kids I worry about, not me.

They passed telephone poles, houses, trees, people, fields, buildings and buildings, took lefts and rights, and lefts and rights. It looked like every place in this country she had ever

187

been, and she knew if she'd tried this drive on her own she most certainly would have got lost. She thought, I know and I don't know where I am, maybe. She knew and she didn't know. New places were just enough different to make her feel unsure of everything, even the familiar. In her mind, prejudice manifested itself as variously as vegetation from region to region. In the West it may be as pallid as the horizon; in the East, as thick and complex as a Pennsylvania wood. It grew everywhere, abundant, dense, floral, prickly; it grew in broad, flat jungle leaves, and in lichen scabs upon stones. In no case could her family escape it, and in perhaps half these places, could scarcely recognize it. But it was always there, one way or the other. A neighbor's smile might be a rose, or a flytrap— it took time to tell—and it got so that Portia learned to assume only two things about white people: nothing and everything.

When she was a girl, prejudice was mostly hearsay. Whites were scarcely real to her, though Taylor, Texas, was about as black as it was white. But she'd grown up behind the fence of the color bar, and the hedge of her father and four older brothers—four stonemasons and a mechanic. Mrs. Winters died when Portia was three, and though Hubert Winters remarried and had two more boys with his new wife, Lucy, whom they called Little-Mama, Portia's family continued to think Portia its baby. All her life, even now, they called her Gal Baby, even the younger two, and before Anton could change her name to Mrs. Oates, he had to prove himself a man to each and every one of the Winters men. They arm wrestled him, challenged him to foot races, interrogated him, slyly, offhandedly, about engine repair, fishing, baseball, his "people." They watched how he handled tools, how he handled ridicule. Anton always responded with humility and good nature, and it annoyed Portia that no one in her family responded in like manner to him.

The day Anton asked Hubert Winters for her hand, Hubert said to Gal Baby, "Yes I did. I told him yes." Portia remembered how he didn't look at her, but at the disassembled clock on the kitchen table before him. Because Anton was asked to wait for Portia in the family room, the room adjacent to the kitchen, Mr. Winters kept his voice low. He edged his glasses up his nose, picked up a gear and frowned. One of her brothers ran a lawn mower past the open kitchen window, and Hubert waited until its clatter died away. "But I also told him that the army belongs to the white man, and that being the case, he do, too. . . . Now." He laid the gear down. "Now I believe in rendering unto Caesar, but I won't be no slave. As I see it, the army ain't hardly differ'nt from slavery, truth be told, and I didn't raise no chir'en to be no slaves, or to marry no slave.

"I told that young man out there that you belong to us and nobody else, not the army, nor the air force, nor navy, nor Marines. I told him he got to keep you home no matter how far from Taylor he take you." He looked up briefly at her face, but not into her eyes. "You understand me?"

Portia didn't understand, but was afraid to say anything but "Yes sir."

Hubert nodded, looked down at the table again and said, "You see, I been blessed with two good wives, and so I know twice as much about marriage as your young man do. Four times, more like. See, I know that when a woman marry a man, *he* marry *her* right back. I was raised as a boy on Winters cooking, but sustained as a man on Walker cooking and Grant cooking. When I look at you and my boys I don't just see

Winters hair and Winters color, but Walker and Grant color, Walker and Grant hair. I told that young man that you not only taking the name Oates, but he taking the name Winters. He belong to us, as much as you his.

"His job is to do what I've spent eighteen years doing. To keep you safe from all harm, all trouble, just as sure as if his name was Winters. His job is to put a wall around you like he was raised a mason. His job is to feed you, and give you every thing in this world you need and deserve. And one more thing: His job is to knock down any man, white or colored, military or no, who lay one finger on you. Don't nobody mess with the Winters people because we been our own people since 1821, and we will stay our own. We do for ourselves, call no man sir, but Jesus. We build our own, break our own. We feed ourselves, defend ourselves. I told that boy that if he don't do right by you, it'll take his whole army to keep me from killing him dead."

"Daddy!"

"I'm not playing."

"I'll be fine."

"I know you will."

"He's a good man."

"Otherwise, I'da said no."

"No wonder he looked so pale."

"Nope, ain't no wonder." He started to grin, then let go and laughed. They both laughed, struggling to keep their noise down. "Daddy, you are terrible," Portia whispered. Her tears weren't only from laughter, but from relief and joy. She wouldn't have married without his blessing, but would have fought for one had she been refused. "Just terrible," she said again.

"You know it's true, Gal Baby." He slipped off his glasses, pinched the bridge of his nose, smoothed tears across his right cheek.

"Poor baby," said Portia.

Finally, he looked her in the eye. "Poor man," he said, his expression growing more sober by degrees. "He's a man, Gal Baby. That's all I'm asking of him. Just that he be a man. His own man, and take good care of you. Little-Mama says the same thing. Just so he take care of you."

Anton did, he always had, wherever military life took them, though she liked few of these places it took them. It annoyed her that Anton adjusted so easily to new places. He loved movement, so military life suited him as though invented for him. As a boy, he'd educated himself on *National Geographic*s, helped support his mother, his sister and himself with any job that permitted him travel: delivering papers, milk, groceries— collecting rags, rent, garbage. Twice in their marriage, Portia had felt compelled to threaten to leave him. Once was for his volunteering for duty in Vietnam. She knew it would help his career, but she also knew it was because Vietnam was one more place he wanted to see. There were times that the mere sight of his globes, his maps, his *Geographic*s was enough to drive her into violent anger, or days of cold silence.

The second threat to leave him came when she realized the extent of his drinking problem. Having grown up in a dry state, and surrounded by abstemious family, she seldom saw alcohol, let alone drunkenness. The first and only time she'd seen a drunk person in her entire girlhood was when she was fifteen or sixteen celebrating Juneteenth on the grounds of Most Precious Lamb Baptist Church. She watched a dark, fat man in a pale green zoot suit as he stood watching the ball game in the field. He weaved from heel to toe, shouting, laughing at nothing Portia could see. He seemed to be rooting for both teams, or rooting for some invisible team beyond the field. Every so often his red eyes would grow big, he'd tip his head back, then abruptly bend at the waist and vomit. All Portia could conclude of the fat man's staggering, his vomiting, his bloody eyes was that he was ill. So it shocked her when her brother T.C. and one of the deacons, Brother Iverson, roughly grabbed the man under the arms, hauled him to Brother Iverson's Ford, and drove him away. Usually, if someone grew sick from all the food, too much heat and laughter, a half-dozen women would descend upon him or her with salves, or sodas, oils, bitter black liquids. But they took this man away as though he carried some catching disease that could kill them all. She asked every adult she knew and trusted what was wrong with the man, and they all confirmed what she had thought, "Sick, Gal Baby," but when she asked why no one had offered him medicine or comfort, they answered in metaphors that made no sense to her till she had been married to Anton for a year. Anton's drinking frightened her because, she believed, it softened him to the core like some horrible cancer. He drank germs, viruses, bugs that made him bloody-eyed and clumsy, laid him out like a man on his sickbed.

He drank only rarely, but there was no rhythm, no regularity to it. It didn't seem precipitated by trouble at work or home, was preceded by no particular mood. It could be once in a month, or three days a week, any time at all, and because this was so, she was always half on alert, always at least half prepared to take over, be a double Winters, and twice the Oates he could be. She felt like a half widow, a double person, both father and mother, an orphan, both officer and troop. When he's there, he's there.

When he's gone, it's just me. It's hard. I don't know what to do half the time. I take lefts when it should be rights. Sometimes I can get there, but can't get back. I don't know maps like he does. I can't remember if the sun sets in the east or the west. I get lost in new quarters, let alone towns. Go left when I should go right. Hallway light on the wrong side. Thought this hallway led to the kitchen, and not the laundry. Didn't teach me to drive till Alva was born. Never needed to drive. With Daddy and them I didn't have to drive or work, 'cept at home. Supposed to have gone to college. Baylor. Interior decorator. Librarian. Nurse. That sort of thing. But I don't like blood. Interior decorator. Little-Mama said, "Send her to Baylor, so she can do for herself. Can't no colored girl to do for herself if she up under a white man's roof with a broom in her hand." But Anton looked like Paul Newman in that uniform. Forget Baylor. Decorate my own house. Arms like Sugar Ray. I want babies with eyes like that. Baby boys, boy babies. Strong like a Winters, green-eyed like an Oates. Men, a wall of 'em. Eyes that see in the darkest places. Everywhere. Traveled everywhere: Korea, Germany, Italy. The north, the south; seen mountains and snow, jungles, oceans, flown way high up in the air. Take me up there with him. Eyes that see everything, everywhere. He's a man, all right. More than half the time, anyway.

Portia leaned forward, lifted her purse to her lap and snapped it open. "I'd like to give you gas money," she said, but Tonya flat refused it. Portia didn't have the will to palaver. She wants to be Christian, let her. I'd have got lost out here, no doubt. All looks the same to me.

The trip turned out to be little more successful than the trip to the base exchange. They gathered dirty looks in practically every store they entered. The clerks (coldly) addressed Tonya only, and their stocks were no more fashionable than those on base. The whole city seemed five, maybe ten years behind the times, and the three of them laughed a lot about the antiquity. Tonya promised, after the first two stores, that she was going to ask the clerk to lead her to the bustle department, and Portia actually did ask one clerk for spats. They laughed so hard, the clerk strode away from them livid with irritation. He asked Tonya to take her "little entourage" elsewhere. After this Alva couldn't keep from pointing out every water fountain and rest room where one could still read the words "For Whites," "Whites Only" or "Colored." And finally, Portia said, from a tight mouth, "Honey, all that stuff is over with. Let it be."

They found adequate underthings for Alva, and pants for Derrick, but Alva decided to think about the pumps Portia offered to buy her. They had a late lunch, on Tonya, at Popeye's Fried Chicken and made it back to Barksdale at about half past six. Portia decided that she definitely liked Tonya Hooker, but just when she hoped she wouldn't ask again about the fishing trip, Tonya said, "The boys would like to pick up Derrick about six, next Saturday. That sound good?"

Portia hesitated for a breath, and said, "We'll see. Lemme talk to Anton."

i x

sunday, monday, tuesday

There was only one time Sergeant Oates varied from his inclinations in disciplining his children. Only one time he behaved as impulsively as Portia seemed to. It was in 1962, when the Oateses were on vacation, visiting family in Tennessee. It had been a tense, uncomfortable visit for the five of them. Dean was suffering from croup, Alva kicked one of her cousins in the rump, and Portia had scalded her leg on coffee fifteen minutes outside of Tullahoma, and because she was in pain, and busy with Dean, she was as much fun as a wet hen, as the old people say. The worst thing happened at the hands of Derrick on the second day home. Anton never figured out how he did so, but Derrick destroyed several dozen glasses, bowls, saucers and cups when he somehow caused a china cabinet to crash to the floor.

When Anton and the other adults entered the dining room to discover the source of the enormous clatter, he felt himself rattled by an embarrassment, a fury, an astonishment that he'd rarely felt outside of work. He felt hot from his throat to his forehead, and there were tears of rage in his eyes. He strode up to Derrick, heedless of the broken glass beneath his stocking feet, grabbed the boy by the scruff and jerked him out the room. He led him outside and to the middle of the bare dirt yard where the chickens fed. "Don't move," he said, and walked to the decrepit toolshed at the end of the carport. His wife and mother stood several feet from Derrick, as if afraid to come any nearer. The rest of the family stood at the kitchen window and watched Anton root through the garage, open boxes, toss them aside. The sergeant found an old waffle iron, and with jittery hands, clamped the iron between his left arm and side, and with his right hand gripped the cord and jerked it from the iron as easily as pulling a stem from an apple.

The blood was so hot and fast in his head that he couldn't

hear the boy scream; he couldn't hear the whistle of the cord in the air or its crack against the boy's flesh. He didn't think of it as flesh. It was more like everything wrong in the world. It took him over a minute to hear his mother's and wife's voices demanding he stop, and if not for his mother throwing her arm around his neck and hollering, an inch from his ear, "Anton, you stop it right now!" he might have beat the boy till he or the boy fell dead. There had been no threats that time, neither had there been the rhetoric, the cross-examinations, the philosophical justifications. There had been only a red light flickering in his peripheral vision, and cloudy black spheres going off like black strobe flashes in his eyes. Thirty minutes after the beating he sat in the kitchen ashen, angry, trembling, still half deaf.

He stopped whipping the children for about a year after that one, and wouldn't have taken up the task again, if not for his belief that to do otherwise was to abrogate one's parental duties. It was unpleasant business to him, but you could no more shirk it than you could earning a wage, or satisfying your wife. But enough is enough, and things change. After Vietnam, he had had enough screaming, enough noise. He just couldn't hit them anymore. Dean didn't seem to need it; Alva was a young woman now, and Derrick, as long as he brought home Cs, and stayed out of trouble, all he needed now was the threat of a whipping and he'd leap like a flea.

He wasn't a bad boy, just strange. Can't sit still for days, then spends days hardly moving, staring into space. No sense of direction, can't remember anything, lazy, up all night. And sleep all day, if you let him. How can a twelve-year-old boy forget to comb his hair? How come he can't use a rake to save his life? No interest in sports. Afraid of water. Destructive.

Always sneaking. Tried to steal my own pocketknife off my own dresser, like I wouldn't know. Mind always someplace else. How many times you got to teach a boy to tie a sheep shank? How can a boy smart as he is do so bad in school? Good fishing partner, though, and can keep a secret, if you ax him to. Respectful to his elders, and don't sneak cigarettes or touch the liquor. Good sense of humor. Naw, all and all, he's a good boy. Just funny.

Still, Sergeant Oates didn't know what to think about the fishing trip that white boy wanted to take him on. It wasn't that he didn't think Derrick deserved to go. He'd done nothing wrong, lately. It's just he worried that Derrick might do something to embarrass him. He didn't know these people, didn't even really like them, and if he were to pull one of his strange stunts, what would they think of him? Sergeant Anton Sutton Oates. Like most parents, he found it hard to separate himself from his children, but he was no pathological case. He knew Derrick liked the boy, and white or not, he was his son's friend, and kids need friends. He didn't know what to say, and Derrick needed some sort of answer, the Hookers had said, by tomorrow. He just didn't know them well, but Portia knew and liked the woman. He assumed they would be spending a good deal of time together, during the day, and even on weekends, now that Alva had become so distant and moody.

But Hooker was another matter to Anton. He despised him the moment he'd laid eyes on him. Anton was an exceedingly intelligent man, but had suffered from race hatred in his early years in the service, and had spent his eighteen years in the air force as a loadmaster, an important enough job, but one far beneath his skills, abilities and ambitions. He had always wanted to be accepted into flight school, and be promoted to warrant officer. He had thought his distinguished service in Vietnam would lead to these deferred ambitions, but he returned still a loadmaster, still a technical sergeant. His sensitivities about these things taught him how to instantly distinguish between would-be allies and men like Hooker. It lay beneath the skin like an insect larva in a chrysalis. A certain sourness in the smile, a gaze that coolly lingered, and lifted the brows just so, a tendency to refer to you by neither your first nor your last name, but by your rank. Got the look of a redneck peckerwood from top to bottom. How many times I seen that face? How many times I had to stand at attention while that face was staring into mine, barking orders, telling me why I ain't gonna be promoted, telling me where I do and don't belong? Or telling me every damn thing but what he really think.

They had nothing to say to each other. The man was a mechanic, Anton knew, and they saw each other on the field, from time to time, but merely nodded when they met, moved on without much more than that.

Sergeant Oates had been staring into the paper while mulling these things over. It was Sunday, and lately, Sunday after church was the only time he had for newspapers, his astronomy, history, geography and botany books. He'd been too busy studying for the senior NCO exam he was to take at the beginning of next quarter. He studied four hours a day, Saturdays and Sundays, and it was all he had time to plumb with any depth. He certainly didn't want to devote his time to this matter with Derrick and the fishing trip. Portia was a better judge of people, as far as he was concerned, and if she said they were all right, then they were. It was that simple. He didn't exactly like the feel of it, but kids need friends. No getting around that.

He can go.

"You can?"

"Yep."

"Neat. Like my dad says, you don't have to bring nothing. No fishing stuff, no knife, no food, no matches, no nothing, except clothes."

"Shoot! I gotta bring clothes?"

"Yeah, a suit."

"A birthday suit."

"A zoot suit."

"You guys got a boat?"

"They got 'em there, and they got worms and everything."

"We could dig for worms."

"Where?"

"In our gardens, after school."

"Today?"

"Why not?"

"You got a shovel?"

"Don't you?"

"We better use yours."

"How come?"

"My dad don't loan his tools."

"So, you use yours, and I'll use mine."

"That's the way it'll *have* to be."

"Okay, okay, don't get cranky."

"I'm—never mind."

"What? What?"

"Never mind, never mind . . . never mind."

The boys said nothing for a spell. Derrick watched three girls jumping rope, Wendy Byrd and a girl named Mary at the ends, and Vera Lawrence skipping. They stood too far from the girls to catch Vera's rhyme, but Derrick imagined *three, six, nine/the goose drank wine/the monkey chewed tobacco on the street car line,* as he watched Vera's lank hair spring six inches off her shoulders and fall back down. Garret looked at the ground. He gazed at but didn't see a liver-colored stone between his feet, but he did notice his right shoe had come unlaced. He could feel his teeth clamped tight, and he could feel his heartbeat in his throat. He knelt to retie his shoe, and when he stood, he heard Derrick say, ". . . Vera?"

"What?"

"What do think of her? I mean, do you like her?"

Garret looked at her and said, "Why would I like her?"

"I think she's nice, that's all."

"She wears the same dress every day."

Derrick shrugged. "Maybe she's poor," he said.

"You think so?"

"Maybe. My dad said he was poor when he was a kid. He didn't have a lot of clothes." Derrick looked at Garret, noted the way he was standing, his arms wrapped around himself, his head bent low, his legs together and curved back like longbows. He wanted to do something to pull Garret out of himself, but his mood seemed too delicate to disturb. He returned to looking at Vera, and said, "She yelled at Stanley and Buck and those guys once when they were calling me names. Told on 'em, too."

"What'd they call you?"

"What you think they called me?"

"Oh. I heard about that. That's when I had the flu."

Garret looked at two boys from his class playing tetherball as two others waited their turn. He hated the game, but wished he could just walk away from Derrick and join them, laugh and holler like them, curse, spit, pick fights, but he could scarcely move today. He wished something would happen to end this recess or at least this moment—a whistle blast, a gust of wind, someone shouting his name. His chest felt quivery, and he couldn't stop swallowing, audible gulping, like a cartoon character. Finally he said. "My dad was poor, too, that's why he's so strict."

"Mine's strict, too."

"Well, not like my dad."

"How would you know?"

" 'Cause I just know! He's tough. And he doesn't play around. He'd do anything to anybody, if he's mad enough. I seen him break a door down once, and once, when Junior pushed Mom down the stairs, Dad tied him to a chair in our garage and slapped him till Mom and me made him stop. And one time he made Devon put the gloves on with him—um, Dad and Devon put the gloves on—and box him once when Devon lied about how the bathroom sink got broke in England one time. He's tough. You cross him and you're dead, you're gone. You see what I'm saying?" He paused only long enough to inhale, then said, "The thing you don't know is that he's stricter than anyone I know. He's not lazy, okay? and he doesn't do what your dad does, because he had a different life than yours. He argued with his dad about cars. Did your dad do that?"

"I don't know."

"See? See? They're different, okay?"

Finally the bell did ring. Garret spun toward the building and walked away. His hands were thrust in his pockets, and he appeared to be walking on his toes. He got in line just behind Vera Lawrence, oddly enough, and as Derrick moved toward the line he alternately looked at the two and imagined them holding hands. Then he imagined himself holding her hand. Then he thought of Garret tied to a chair as his father backhanded him. For some reason he imagined Garret to be Junior's age, and he imagined him slipping from his bonds and cold-cocking the bear man with a single blow; then Derrick and his wife, Vera, would hide him in their basement until the trouble blew over. They would live together for a long time this way, cutting the grass together, playing football, their wives talking on the porch, their kids on bikes or jumping rope—*the line broke/the monkey got choked/and they all went to heaven in a little row boat.* These thoughts kept him from seeing how angry he was, and how uneasy. He shrugged away his silly thoughts and got in line.

Junior and Devon Hooker were being grounded for teasing Alva Oates at the bus stop at school on Tuesday morning. They were allowed no television, no Cokes, and no dessert. They were to stay in their room, do homework, speak in whispers. At lights out, they were to be in their bunks. Ordinarily, when on restrictions, they could listen to the radio, because neither of them could sleep without it, but it had to be kept on very low, and their mother got to choose the station. But this time, Tonya had been so angry that she disallowed them the radio, and they lay in their beds, fulminating in low tones. "Shit," said Junior, "I'm still hungry."

Devon said, "If it'd been up to Dad, we'd a been able to have seconds."

"She was mad, whudn't she?"

"Could you believe that shit? I thought she was gonna kick us out. Man, when she threw that glass I thought she surely must have lost her mind."

"She lost it, all right."

They were quiet for a while, and Devon thought Junior had fallen asleep. He could fall asleep in a blink, anywhere and anytime he was tired enough. One minute he was telling you something he felt was important, the next he was speaking in tongues, giggling to himself, smacking his lips like a baby. He didn't want Junior to be asleep. He wanted to talk to him about sex, about the things he was feeling for Alva. He hadn't meant to tease her. It hadn't even crossed his mind. If Junior were awake, and Devon could find the courage, he'd say things like, After all, Dad said that colored girls aren't like the men. He said they weren't as bad. They work hard, he said, and it must be true because she makes good grades. And she's pretty, Junior, she's so pretty. She's colored, but she's the color of caramel and I like caramel. When she looks into my eyes it's like something scooping out my stomach. No, no, that's not right, it's like when you take me driving, and we swoop off the overpass, and you're doing, like, sixty, and we come down that hill with the apple trees? You know how your stomach gets that . . . And like her face. I'm always looking at her face. She doesn't talk like, you know, "Hey, ma-a-a-n, you be goin' to da show?" you know, like other ones do. Her breath smells like celery and apples. She watches *The Prisoner*, Junior. You know how hard it is to find a girl who's even heard of that show?

He didn't know how he was going to get at the things he wanted to say, and if he waited too long, Junior was sure to fall asleep. Devon wasn't as good at talking as Junior and Garret. He couldn't make things clear with words. Except with Alva. The only hard part about talking to her was making it look like he didn't care, and coming up with some excuse to talk to her. This morning, for example, she had been standing at the bus stop early, as Devon always did. He believed she had come out early to be alone with him. After they'd exchanged hellos, they remained silent for what seemed to Devon a long time, and it was, to him, considering that soon the other kids would arrive, including Junior, who would give him the arched brow, the suspecting smirk. The fat colored girl would come, too, and take Alva by the arm, walk her a few feet away from all the white kids at the stop, and start in with all the whispering, pointing, laughing, things that clearly annoyed and embarassed Alva.

He had had to say something, anything, soon, to Alva, so he said, "Did you see Ed Sullivan the other night?" She said she had, so he said, "Uh, they had that guy on there, that singer."

"Ray Stevens," she said.

"Yeah. Did you like that song?"

"The first one, yeah. 'Everything Is Beautiful.' "

"Yeah, the second one was terrible."

And before he knew it, Junior had smacked his hat off from behind, and kicked him when he bent over to pick it up. Junior didn't kick him hard, and he didn't fall, but he'd never felt more humiliation in his life. When Alva handed him his hat, he wouldn't even look at her hand. "Say thank you,"

Junior sang. And Peter Clovis said, "Say thank you, ma'am." Then some senior said, "Mammy, say 'Mammy'!" And someone else said Aunt Je-mammy, and it got worse. Devon didn't even know how to defend her, because all the cracks were directed at him. He felt frozen with anger, mortification, guilt, confusion. Then Junior started bobbing and weaving in front of Devon like a boxer, a ridiculous boxer, bouncing, pumping his arms, sniffing and snorting, punching his own chin and staggering. "Come on, Sport. Lemme warm up on ya." It was a family joke, an inside joke the Hookers had always used to defuse tension, and it made Devon laugh. It was a small laugh, but it was enough to draw him from her side to his. Though he caught himself, made his face reveal a sober annoyance, it was too late, for when he turned to look at Alva, she was standing with the fat colored girl, who had her arm round Alva's shoulder, and cut him a look that ought to have made his blood spill.

"Junior?" said Devon.

"Speak."

"Thought you were asleep."

"Speak."

"Tell me again why we're doing what we're doing on Saturday."

"You mean the fishing trip? Whadda you mean, 'why'? You know damn well why."

"I mean, what exactly are we gonna do?"

"Lynch the bastard."

Devon kicked the bottom of his brother's mattress, and Junior giggled. "I'm serious, June."

"We just scare the shit out of him. No one gets hurt."

"Well, why isn't Sonny in on it? He thinks—"

"You think I don't know that? I know what he thinks. If he knew, he'd tell Derrick. Right now, he's too scared to say anything. See, if he thinks it's all a joke, he'll squeak, but the way it is now, it's all such a big deal, he feels like if he says anything he'll get the whole family thrown in jail."

Devon was quiet for a moment; then he said, "You still awake?"

"Speak."

"This whole thing seems like a waste of time, and it sounds boring. I'm not going."

"What?"

"I'm not."

"Yeah, like you got a choice."

"What's he gonna do, kill me?"

"If he's in a good mood, yeah."

"It sounds stupid."

"I know what it is. You're scared."

"That's got nothing to do with it."

"Scared."

"Eat me."

"Well, I *am* hungry."

"Fuck you, Eugene; I'm not interested. I'm not going."

"Oh come on, man, don't be scared. There's nothing to be scared about. Hell, if I don't bring my grades up, I could be in Vietnam in ten, twelve months. Now, that's scary. All this shit we're doing? This whole 'fishing trip'? This'll be fun. Man, Dad's got sheets, rope, gasoline. We're gonna do it up. Then, when the guy's eyes pop out his skull, and he turns white, we tell him we've changed our minds—for now—but if he doesn't start hanging out with his own kind, we'll bring him back there and cook him, fucking nigger. We untie him and tell him what to tell his folks and everybody goes home. Nobody gets hurt. Simple."

"Sounds stupid," said Devon, and he rolled onto his side, propping his head in his palm. "What if Derrick tells anyway. I mean, what if he tells his sister, or something? You know, not his parents, but his sister, and *she* tells their parents. You know what Mom'll do, if she finds out? You think she was bad tonight? It's not worth it. What Dad should just tell Garret is that he can't be friends with Derrick. I mean, doesn't that make more sense?

"Junior, don't you think that makes more sense?

"Junior?

"Junior, you awake?"

X

love life

On Friday morning it was cool and clear, and Derrick believed the weather tomorrow would be just as nice. They wouldn't be on the bus, but in Sergeant Hooker's Rambler, and they'd be half asleep shivering off the cold as they scooted down the road in the dark. Perfect fishing weather, the kind where the horizon, at five-thirty in the morning, would be pink as salmon flesh and the shallows of the lake would be capped with the thinnest, clearest ice. The middle of the lake would be black and still. The sun would ease up over the water, steam would peel off and lift away, and the air would smell of wet wood, bitter leaves, clover, fish, Dad's coffee, the fried bologna sandwiches in their greasy bags, and it would all mix together sweet and solid as something you could hold in your hands. Birds would make the only sound, except Dad's rumbling voice as he said, "See them rings? They're rising. Cast that way." Sometimes on the nights after they'd been out all day, Derrick would close his eyes, and he'd see a red-and-white bobber plunge into the black in which it floated. His body would jerk him awake. He could almost feel the pole in his hands.

No Friday ever felt so good to him. It had been a bad week. Stanley Dumonde had fired spit wads at him at Tuesday lunch, and when he told Mrs. Wafer, she popped her fingers at Stanley and said it was childish and unsanitary. "Go sit down," she said to Derrick. Alva had had some trouble at school that day which she told only Mom about. And Dean had been suspended from school for beating some boy who had called him a coon. As usual, his mother found a way to blame Derrick. She said he should be looking out for his brother since he'd just had stitches. On Wednesday, Mrs. Wafer had paddled him in the teacher's lounge for taking an arithmetic test with a red ink pen, and for forgetting his homework. And on the same day, James Melvin kept pestering Derrick by asking him whether Derrick was his "pal." Because of the way Melvin emphasized the word, Derrick was immediately suspicious, so he wouldn't give in to Melvin no matter how hard Melvin pressed him. "I'm your friend," Derrick said, "your buddy, your amigo—"

"But are you my *pal*?" Melvin grinned so nastily that Derrick felt disgust.

"Why?"

"Are you?"

It went on like this for every moment of morning recess, and Derrick was angry enough to slap Melvin, but instead he went to Mrs. Wafer, to tell on Melvin, and she shaped every wrinkle in her face to reflect her irritation. "Nobody likes a tattletale, Durrick," she said, and threatened to keep him after school if he couldn't act more maturely. Even Garret had been difficult lately. He had barely spoken all week; his enthusiasm about the fishing trip decreased to the point of indifference, and Derrick couldn't remember Garret looking him in the eye since Monday. Every day of the week, Derrick reminded him that they had to dig worms, and Garret went from making lame excuses to shrugs and rolling eyes. "We can buy worms there," Garret said.

"But ours are for free," Derrick said, "and it's fun. My Dad said he might let us hot-wire 'em. You ever done that?" Garret simply wouldn't answer. He acted the same way Thursday, and from the look of him, he'd be the same way today.

He sat beside Derrick, but practically smashed his face against the window. His hands were shoved deep into his pockets, and he pressed his knees against the milky green bulkhead of the bus. His blush was so deep, you'd think his father had backhanded him this morning. He looked sleepily put out whenever Derrick asked him a question. But Garret could be moody, could even cry for no detectable reason, if you didn't know him. Derrick didn't know Garret as well as he'd known Jerry Thomas, Ricky Hardy or Eddie Lopez, his best friends in California, Colorado and Texas, but he had what they had. They talked, and you felt as though *you* were talking; they listened, and you felt they absorbed every word you said, that they could have, if they wanted to, spoken every word you were saying, as you said them; they walked silently with you on a field or in the woods, and it was as though you were still talking. Their gaze fell on the same things yours did, but at the same time, they could show you something new in things you'd seen all your life.

When Derrick finally got up enough resentment to demand that Garret stop staring at him, on his second day at Waller, he was surprised at the fear in Garret's eyes. When Derrick returned the stare that day, he'd expected to see a bully's squint, but instead Garret's eyes evinced shock, and he blushed so intensely that Derrick almost laughed. "Why you keep staring at me?"

"You live next door to me," said Garret. Derrick thought he saw the redhead's bottom lip trembling, but he wouldn't let himself believe it. He had never frightened anyone in his life. They had just been dismissed for lunch, and were stowing their books in their desk cubbies. James Melvin stepped in front of Garret and elbowed past Derrick, saying, "Hey, pals, you my pals?" He grinned and stepped out of the room. His exit left Garret and Derrick alone in the classroom, except for Mrs. Wafer, who was at her desk, scribbling furiously.

"I know where you live," Derrick said.

"We ride the same bus."

"You don't think I've seen you?"

"I know." Garret's blush deepened, and he took a backward step.

"So why do you keep telling me stuff I know?"

"I didn't think you noticed me. You never look up."

This intrigued Derrick, and it even unsettled him, a little. What's he mean I don't look up? I look up. Are you kidding? How could I walk around if I didn't look up sometimes? But the more he tossed these things around in his mind, the more he was thrown back on himself. He could see how he walked, or at least see what he observed when he walked. He saw floors, sidewalks, flower beds and gardens. Where his eyes fell he found jackknives, pennies, five-dollar bills. Dean had always considered Derrick lucky because he could find things everywhere they went. The top of his dresser drawer was littered with crushed bottle tops, feathers, quartz stones, dirt-encrusted marbles, wild bird eggshells, jacks, rusty screws, nuts, bolts, washers, springs. He found nothing in the crooks of trees, nothing at nose level. He remembered his old friends' shoes and knees as well as he could remember their eyes: Jerry's scuffed Buster Browns; Rick's orange hiking boots with the mini-flashlight in the pocket; Eddie's black Converse high-tops with the grass-stained toes.

The reverie flashed through his mind in a second, and he looked Garret in the eye. He felt he recognized him. "So how long have you lived here?" he said. Garret answered him, and they left the room together, talking. They sat together at lunch, met at afternoon recess, sat together on the bus, and all the while they talked. From that day forward, Garret and Derrick spent all their free time at school together, but Garret was always standoffish and reserved at home. Derrick assumed that this was just Garret's way. But Garret had never been as reserved at home as he was this morning. Derrick wanted to ask him what was bothering him, but he seemed closed even to that.

He hated this distance, but didn't know whether to lose his temper or worry. He wanted to talk to Garret about all the fish they would catch, the fun they could have, even if the fishing was bad. We could set rabbit traps, or use hotdog pieces and string to catch crawdads. We could go to a place no one was fishing and skip rocks; we could talk for hours, or be quiet. We could make bows and arrows and shoot at old cans and bottles, or play mumblety-peg, or wade. We could play anything, do anything, and it would be all right as long as you don't act like a jerk like you're acting now, and as long as you don't get sick.

The bus stopped. Everyone got off in the slow, stiff way of Mondays and Fridays, but Derrick felt that Garret wasn't directly behind him, and he turned around. Sure enough, Garret remained in his seat, hunched into himself in the same way he'd been for the entire ride. The movement of the other children carried Derrick along until he was off the bus, but he stood by the door and waited for Garret, but it appeared that either Garret had walked by him and he hadn't noticed, or that he was still on the bus. He checked the back of every head that moved away from the bus. When he heard the bus driver say, "You sick, young man?" he stepped back onto the bus and past the driver, before she was even out of her seat. "He your friend? You know him?" the driver said.

"Yes ma'am. I live next door to him."

"You sick, young man?" the driver said again, but Garret wouldn't answer.

"I'll go see," said Derrick, and the driver left the bus, saying she was going to find the school nurse.

Garret did look sick. His face was now pale, his lips dry, his hair dark with perspiration. Derrick reached out a hand to touch Garret on the forehead, but Garret shot his own hand up and grabbed Derrick by the wrist. "Guess what, Derrick?"

"Huh?"

"I said, 'Guess what.'" Garret was smiling, and his eyes looked deep and dark, rimmed with red.

"What?"

"You're a nigger and I'm not."

Derrick felt a great wheel roll so low and heavy through his gut that his knees buckled. He pulled his arm from Garret's grip. He swallowed, squinted, smiled uncertainly. "What? What did you say?"

"Let's try not to be too stupid today, Derrick. I just told you that you're a nigger and I'm not, okay?"

"What are you doing? What . . . What—"

Garret leaned forward in his seat, clasped the seat back in front of him with both hands, and said, " 'Cause you're a nigger and I'm not. I'm better than you. I was born better, and I'll die better. White people are better than colored people. We used to own you." Then he spat up at Derrick, but missed, and spat again, but hardly anything came out. Derrick felt one cold droplet on his thumb.

"You better be sick," Derrick said, but he could barely get the words out. He steadied his breathing, and again he said, "You better be sick, Garret," but when he said it a second time, the words made no sense to him. He had no idea what he was trying to say.

"Sick of you," said Garret, and he sat back heavily in his seat. "You're a nigger, and I'm not. And if you think you're going fishing tomorrow, Sport, you better see a headshrinker. We hate niggers." Garret rested his head on the seat back, then slowly rolled it left so he was looking out the window. "Black nigger," he said, as if to himself.

Derrick turned away and alighted the bus. He didn't see the front door of the school, couldn't find it for half a minute. He couldn't see the sidewalk, and missed it, started across the dirt toward the second- and third-grade playgrounds, stopped himself, turned left, then left again, but still couldn't find the door. He thought he must have been looking right at it, but he just couldn't see it. Out the corner of his eye, he did see the bus driver and the nurse walking behind him, and he turned to watch them step onto the bus. A few seconds later they were on the sidewalk again, the nurse and the driver to the left and right of Garret, holding him under his arms. Derrick looked Garret in the eye and Garret suddenly bent at the knees and waist. Both women lost their grip on him. He planted both palms on the ground and heaved as though he were passing all his innards, but he gave up only a trickle of saliva. It sounded as though he was bawling, or perhaps coughing; it was a coarse hoot, was the only sound in the school yard.

Derrick turned when he heard Mrs. Wafer calling him. There she was, and there was the door, right in front of him, not ninety feet away. She was calling him, and waving her hand over her head, and from that distance, it almost looked as though she were smiling. It almost looked as though she were a mother waving at her son, whom she loved, and whom she hadn't seen in a long, long time. Derrick looked at the ground, so as not to trip, and ran to her.